W9-AVP-985

RANDOM
HOUSE
LARGE
PRINT

Also by Emma Cline
Available from Random House
Large Print

The Girls

DADDY

DADDY

stories

EMMA CLINE

RANDOM HOUSE
LARGE PRINT

Published in the United States of America by Random House Large Print in association with Random House, an imprint and division of Penguin Random House LLC, New York.

The following stories were previously published: "What Can You Do with a General," "Son of Friedman," and "Northeast Regional" in **The New Yorker;** "Los Angeles" and "Arcadia" in **Granta;** "The Nanny" and "Marion" in **The Paris Review.**

Cover design: Anna Kochman

The Library of Congress has established a Cataloging-in-Publication record for this title.

ISBN: 978-0-593-29518-2

www.penguinrandomhouse.com/large-print-format-books

FIRST LARGE PRINT EDITION

Printed in the United States of America

10 9 8 7 6 5 4 3 2 1

This Large Print edition published in accord with the standards of the N.A.V.H.

CONTENTS

DADDY

WHAT CAN YOU DO WITH A GENERAL

LINDA WAS INSIDE, ON HER PHONE— to who, this early? From the hot tub, John watched her pace in her robe and an old swimsuit in a faded tropical print that probably belonged to one of the girls. It was nice to drift a little in the water, to glide to the other side of the tub, holding his coffee above the waterline, the jets churning away. The fig tree was bare, had been for a month now, but the persimmon trees were full. The kids should bake cookies when they get here, he thought, persimmon cookies. Wasn't that what Linda used to make, when the kids were little? Or what else—jam, maybe? All this fruit going to waste, it was disgusting. He'd get the yard guy to pick a few crates of persimmons before the kids came, so that all they'd have to do was bake them. Linda would know where to find the recipe.

The screen door banged. Linda folded her robe, climbed into the hot tub.

"Sasha's flight's delayed."

"Till?"

"Probably won't land until four or five."

Holiday traffic would be a nightmare then, coming back from the airport—an hour there, then two hours back, if not more. Sasha didn't have her license, couldn't rent a car, not that she would think to offer.

"And she said Andrew's not coming," Linda said, making a face. Linda was convinced that Sasha's boyfriend was married, though she'd never brought it up with Sasha.

Linda fished a leaf out of the water and flicked it into the yard, then settled in with the book she'd brought. Linda read a lot: She read books about angels and saints and rich white women from the past with eccentric habits. She read books by the mothers of school shooters and books by healers who said that cancer was really a self-love problem. Now it was a memoir by a girl who'd been kidnapped at the age of eleven. Held in a backyard shed for almost ten years.

"Her teeth were in good shape," Linda said. "Considering. She says she scraped her teeth every night with her fingernails. Then he finally gave her a toothbrush."

"Jesus," John said, what seemed like the right response, but Linda was already back to her book, bobbing peacefully. When the jets turned off, John waded over in silence to turn them on again.

Sam was the first of the kids to arrive, driving up from Milpitas in the certified preowned sedan he had purchased the summer before. He had called multiple times before buying the car to weigh the pros and cons—the mileage on this used model versus leasing a newer one and how soon Audis needed servicing—and it amazed John that Linda had time for this, their thirty-year-old son's car frettings, but she always took his calls, going into the other room and leaving John wherever he was, alone with whatever he was doing. Lately John had started watching a television show about two older women living together, one uptight, the other a free spirit. The good thing was that there seemed to be an infinite number of episodes, an endless accounting of their mild travails in an unnamed beach town. Time didn't seem to apply to these women, as if they were already dead, though he supposed the show was meant to take place in Santa Barbara.

Chloe arrived next, down from Sacramento, and she had driven, she said, at least half an hour with the gas light on. Maybe longer. She was doing an internship. Unpaid, naturally. They still covered her rent; she was the youngest.

"Where'd you fill up?"

"I didn't yet," she said. "I'll do it later."

"You should've stopped," John said. "It's dangerous to drive on empty. And your front tire is almost flat," he went on, but Chloe wasn't listening. She was already on her knees in the gravel driveway, clutching tight to the dog.

"Oh, my little honey," she said, her glasses fogged up, holding Zero to her chest. "Little dear."

Zero was always shivering, which one of the kids had looked up and said was normal for Jack Russells, but it still unnerved John.

LINDA WENT TO PICK UP Sasha because John wasn't supposed to drive long distances with his back—sitting made it spasm—and, anyway, Linda said she was happy to do it. Happy to get a little time alone with Sasha. Zero tried to follow Linda to the car, bumping against her legs.

"He can't be out without a leash," Linda said. "Be gentle with him, okay?"

John found the leash, careful, when he clipped it to the harness, to avoid touching Zero's raised stitches. They looked spidery, sinister. Zero was breathing hard. For another five weeks, they were supposed to make sure he didn't roll over, didn't jump, didn't run. He had to be on a leash whenever he went outside, had to be accompanied at all times. Otherwise the pacemaker might get knocked loose. John hadn't known dogs could get pacemakers, didn't even like dogs inside the house. Now here he was, shuffling after Zero while he sniffed one tree, then another.

Zero limped slowly to the fence line, stood still for a moment, then kept going. It was two acres, the backyard, big enough that you felt insulated from the neighbors, though one of them had called the police once, because of the dog's barking. These people, up in one another's business, trying to control barking dogs. Zero stopped to consider a deflated soccer ball, so old it looked fossilized, then kept moving. Finally he squatted, miserable, looking back at John as he took a creamy little shit. It was a startling, unnatural green.

Inside the animal was some unseen machinery keeping him alive, keeping his animal heart pumping. Robot dog, John crooned to himself, kicking dirt over the shit.

Four o'clock. Sasha's plane would just be landing, Linda circling arrivals. It was not too early for a glass of wine.

"Chloe? Are you interested?"

She was not. "I'm applying to jobs," she said, cross-legged on her bed. "See?" She turned the laptop toward him for a moment, some document up on the screen, though he heard a TV show playing in the background. She still seemed like a teenager, though she'd graduated college almost two years ago. At her age, John had already been working for Mike, had his own crew by the time he was thirty. He was thirty when Sam was born. Now kids got a whole extra decade to do—what? Float around, do these internships.

He tried again. "Are you sure? We can sit outside, it's not bad."

Chloe didn't look up from the laptop. "Can you close the door," she said, tonelessly.

Sometimes their rudeness left him breathless.

He put together a snack for himself. Shards of cheese, cutting around the mold. Salami. The last of the olives, shriveled in their brine. He took his paper plate outside and sat in one of the patio chairs. The cushions felt damp, probably rotting from the inside. He wore his jeans, his white socks, his white sneakers, a knitted sweater—Linda's—that seemed laughably and obviously a woman's. He didn't worry about that anymore, how silly he might look. Who would care? Zero came to sniff his hand; he fed him a piece of salami. When the dog was calm, quiet, he wasn't so bad. He should put Zero's leash on, but it was inside, and, anyway, Zero seemed mellow, no danger of him running around. The backyard was green, winter green. There was a fire pit under the big oak tree which one of the kids had dug in high school and ringed with rocks, but now it was filled with leaves and trash. Probably Sam, he thought, and shouldn't Sam clean it up, clean all this up? Anger lit him up suddenly, then passed just as quickly. What was he going to do, yell at him? The kids just laughed now if he got angry. Another piece of salami for Zero, a piece for himself. It was cold and tasted like the refrigerator, like the plastic tray it had come on. Zero stared at him with those marble eyes, exhaling his hungry, meaty breath until John shooed him away.

Even accounting for holiday traffic, Linda and Sasha got back later than he expected. He went out onto the porch when he heard their car. He'd had the yard guy put up holiday lights along the fence, along the roof, around the windows. They were these new LED ones, chilly strands of white light dripping off the eaves. It looked nice now, in the first blue dark, but he missed the colored lights of his childhood, those cartoonish bulbs. Red, blue, orange, green. Probably they were toxic.

Sasha opened the passenger door, a purse and an empty water bottle on her lap.

"The airline lost my suitcase," she said. "Sorry, I'm just annoyed. Hi, Dad."

She hugged him with one arm. She looked a little sad, a little fatter than the last time he'd seen her. She was wearing some unflattering style of pant, wide at the legs, and her cheeks were sweating under too much makeup.

"Did you talk to someone?"

"It's fine," she said. "I mean, yeah, I left my information and stuff. I got a claim number, some website. They're never going to find it, I'm sure."

"We'll see," Linda said. "They reimburse you, you know."

"How was traffic?" John asked.

"Backed up all the way to 101," Linda said. "Ridiculous."

If there were luggage, at least he would have something to do with his hands. He gestured in the direction of the driveway, the darkness beyond the porch light.

"Well," he said, "now everyone's here."

"IT'S BETTER THIS WAY," Sam said. "Isn't it better?"

Sam was in the kitchen, connecting Linda's iPad to a speaker he'd brought. "Now you can play any music you want."

"But isn't it broken?" Linda said from the stove. "The iPad? Ask your dad, he knows."

"It's just out of batteries," Sam said. "See? Just plug it in like this."

The counter was cluttered—John's secretary, Margaret, had dropped off a plate of Rocky Road fudge covered in Saran wrap, and old clients had sent a tin of macadamia nuts and a basket of fig spreads that would join the fig spreads from years past, dusty and unopened in the pantry. Lemons in a basket from the trees along the fence line, so many lemons. They should do something with the lemons. At least give some to the yard guy to take home. Chloe was sitting on one of the stools, opening Christmas cards, Zero at her feet.

"Who are these people, anyway?" Chloe held up a card. A photograph of three smiling blond boys in jeans and denim shirts. "They look religious."

"That's your cousin's kids," John said, taking the card. "Haley's boys. They're very nice."

"I didn't say they weren't **nice.**"

"Very smart kids." They had been good boys, the afternoon they visited, the youngest laughing in a crazy way when John dangled him upside down by his ankles.

Linda said that John was being too rough, her voice getting high, whiny. She got worried so easily. He loves it, John said. And it was true: when he righted the boy, his cheeks red, his eyes wild, he'd asked to go again.

Sasha came downstairs: her face was wet from washing, some sulfurous lotion dabbed on her chin. She looked sleepy, unhappy in borrowed sweatpants and a sweatshirt from the college Chloe had gone to. Linda talked to Sam every day, Chloe, too, and saw them often enough, but Sasha hadn't been home since March. Linda was happy, John could tell, happy to have the kids there, everyone in one place.

John announced that it was time for a drink. "Everyone? Yes?" he said. "I think let's do a white."

"What do you want to listen to?" Sam said, controlling the iPad with a finger. "Mom? Any song."

"Christmas songs," Chloe said. "Put on a Christmas station."

Sam ignored her. "Mom?"

"I liked the CD player," Linda said. "I knew how to use it."

"But you can have everything that was on your CDs, and even more," Sam said. "Anything."

"Just pick something and play it," Sasha said. "Christ."

A commercial blared.

"If you subscribe," Sam said, "then there won't be any commercials."

"Come on," Sasha said. "They don't want to deal with that stuff."

Sam, wounded, turned the volume down, studied the iPad in silence. Linda said that she loved the speaker, thank you for setting it up, wasn't it nice how it freed up all this counter space, and dinner was ready anyway so they could just turn the music off.

CHLOE SET THE TABLE: paper napkins, the cloudy drinking glasses. John had to call someone to look at the dishwasher. It wasn't draining properly, and seemed only to marinate the dishes in a stew of warm water and food scraps. Linda sat at the head of the table, the kids in their usual spots. John finished his wine. Linda had stopped drinking, just to try it out, she said, just for a while, and since then he had drunk more, or maybe it only felt that way.

Sasha pinched a leaf of lettuce from the salad bowl and started chewing.

"Excuse you," he said.

"What?"

"We have to say grace."

Sasha made a face.

"I'll say it," Sam said. He closed his eyes, bowed his head.

When John opened his eyes, he saw Sasha

on her phone. The impulse to grab the phone, smash it. But best not to get mad, or Linda would get mad at him, they would all get mad. How easily things got ruined. He refilled his wine, served himself some pasta. Chloe kept reaching down to feed Zero scraps of rotisserie chicken.

Sasha poked at the pasta. "Is there cheese in this?" She made a show of not taking any. There was only wet lettuce and some shreds of chicken on her plate. She sniffed her water glass. "It smells weird."

Linda blinked. "Well, get another glass then."

"Smell," Sasha said, tipping it at Chloe. "See?"

"Get a new glass," Linda said, and snatched it away. "I'll get it."

"Stop, stop, I'll do it, it's fine."

When the kids were little, dinner was hot dogs or spaghetti, the kids with their glasses of milk, Linda drinking white wine with ice cubes, John with his wine, too, tuning in and out. The kids fought. Chloe kicked Sam. Sasha thought Sam was breathing on her—**Mom, tell Sam to stop breathing**

on me. Tell. Sam. To. Stop. Breathing. On. Me. How easily a veil dropped between him and this group of people who were his family. They fuzzed out, pleasantly, became vague enough that he could love them.

"We're sorry Andrew couldn't make it," Linda said.

Sasha shrugged. "He would have had to fly back on Christmas anyway. He has his son the next day."

"Still, we would've liked to see him."

"Zero's being weird," Chloe said. "Look."

There was chicken on the floor in front of the dog but he wasn't eating it.

"He's cyborg now," Sasha said.

"Maybe he can't see?" Chloe said. "Do you know if he's blind?"

"Don't feed him from the table," John said.

"Not like it really matters at this point."

"Don't say that."

"Can you imagine being a dog?" Sasha said. "Being ready to die and then just, like, no, you're cut open and they put something inside you, and you're still alive? Maybe he hates it."

John had had a similar thought out on

one of Zero's shit walks. Zero had looked so mournful, so ill at ease in his harness, hobbling in the wet grass with his pale-pink belly, and it seemed awful, what people did to animals, pressing them into emotional servitude, keeping them alive for one last Christmas. The kids didn't even care about the dog, not really.

"He likes it," Sam said, bending to pet Zero roughly under the chin. "He's happy."

"Gentle, Sammy, gentle."

"Stop, you're hurting him," Chloe said.

"God," Sam said. "Calm down." He sat back hard in his chair so that it scraped the floor.

"You made him mad, look," Chloe said. Zero circled back to the grimy beanbag they used as his bed. The dog settled down in the lump of fake fur, shivering, staring at them.

"He hates us," Sasha said. "So much."

THEY WATCHED THE SAME movie every year. John opened a bottle of red and brought it into the living room, though only he and Sasha were still drinking. Linda made popcorn on the stove, a touch burnt. He felt for the unpopped kernels on the bottom of the bowl, rolled them around his mouth to suck the salt.

"Let's go," he said. "Let's get a move on."

"Are we ready? Where's Sasha?"

Chloe shrugged from the floor. "Talking to Andrew."

The front door opened. When Sasha came into the living room, she looked as if she'd been crying. "I told you guys to start without me."

"You know, Sash, we can take you to get some clothes tomorrow," Linda said. "The mall is still open."

"Maybe," she said. "Yeah." She went to lie next to Chloe on the carpet. Her face was lit by her phone, her fingers tapping away.

The movie was longer than he remembered. He'd forgotten the whole first section, down in Florida, the train escape. That one actor was a faggot, that seemed obvious now. The retired general, the inn, snowy, snowy Vermont—John fell into a lull, all this East Coast hale and heartiness, everyone in ruddy good health. Why had he and Linda stayed in California? Maybe that was the problem, raising kids in this temperate place where they didn't know the seasons. How much better off they'd have been in Vermont or New Hampshire or one of those states where the cost of living was cheap, where the kids could have done 4-H and gone to community college and got used to the idea of a small, good life, which was all he had ever wanted for his children.

The kids used to love movies like this when they were little, those old, live-action Walt Disney movies, **Pollyanna; The One and Only, Genuine, Original Family Band; The Happiest Millionaire.** Movies where the fathers were basically Jesus, the kids crowding around whenever the dad came into a room, hanging off his neck, kissing him, oh Pa-paw, the little girls said, almost swooning. Such great faces, those old actors. Fred MacMurray, the one from **The Music Man.** Or was he thinking of the actor from **Little House on the Prairie,** the boxed set that they'd watched in its entirety? Pa was always shirtless at least once an episode, his feathery hair so deeply seventies. John had read the girls those books when they were young. The Little House books and the book about the boy running away to live in the mountains, the boy running away to live in the woods, books about young people out in holy, unspoiled nature, fording clear brooks, sleeping in beds made of tree boughs.

On-screen, Danny Kaye was singing, the blonde in her pink dress dancing, her great legs, and John hummed along, off key, the dog in the room, he could tell, the harness jangling though he couldn't see the dog, but someone else could take Zero out, one of the kids. That's why Zero was alive, anyway. For them.

He had fallen asleep. The movie was over, but no one had turned the television off. His wineglass was empty. Everyone was gone. They had left him alone. The room was dark but outside the holiday lights were still on, casting a peculiar glow through the windows, an eerie, alien brightness. It occurred suddenly to him that something was wrong. He sat, unmoving, the wineglass in his hand. He remembered this feeling from childhood, the nights he lay paralyzed in his bottom bunk, hardly breathing from fear, convinced that some evil was gathering itself in the silence, gliding soundlessly toward him. And here it was, he thought, finally, it had come for him. As he had always known it would.

A spasm in his back, and the room reoriented itself: the couch, the carpet, the television. Ordinary. He stood up. He put his wineglass on the coffee table, turned out the hallway lights, the kitchen lights, went upstairs where everyone, his family, was sleeping.

THE NEXT DAY WAS Christmas Eve. John carried two cups of coffee up to the bedroom. It was sunny outside, the fog burning off, but the bedroom was dark, Colonial dark, anachronistically dark. Linda had picked the dark wallpaper and the dark curtains and the four-poster bed, and it's not as if John had some vision of what he would have preferred. On the nightstand on his side of the bed: a wooden tray of pennies in the drawer; a shoehorn still in its plastic package; a chubby anthology of crime stories. In the closet, a broken-down device that he had used to hang upside down for twenty minutes a day, good for his back, until Linda said the sight was too frightening.

Linda sat up in bed and took the mug, her sleep shirt twisted up around her neck, her face rumpled. She blinked a few times, groping for her glasses.

"Sasha's awake," he said.

"Was she nasty?"

John shrugged. "She's fine."

"I'm afraid to go downstairs. She was so upset yesterday. About her bag. It really unnerved me."

"She seems fine to me."

Was that true? He didn't know. Sasha saw a therapist, which John was aware of only because Linda paid the health insurance and Sasha was still on their plan. In high school, Sasha had also gone to a therapist, someone who was supposed to help her stop scratching her legs up with tweezers and nail scissors. It didn't seem to do anything but give her new words to describe how awful her parents were.

When the kids were young, Linda had

gone to a ranch in Arizona for a week or so, a health place. He guessed it would have been after one of the bad periods, when she sometimes ended up locking him out of the house, or taking the kids to her mother's. One night, Sasha, nine years old, had called the police on him. When they arrived at the house, Linda told them it was an accident, cleared everything up. It was years ago, he told Linda when she brought it up. And things had changed after that. Linda came back from the health retreat with a book of low-fat recipes that all seemed to use mango salsa, and a conviction that she had communed with the ghost of her childhood dog during a guided meditation in a sweat lodge. And she'd decided that John needed to see a therapist. It was, he supposed, an ultimatum.

He'd gone twice. The man had prescribed him antidepressants and a mood stabilizer, and given him a handout of breathing exercises for impulse control. That first day on the pills he'd felt something like mania, his thoughts a bright crumple of tinfoil—he'd cleaned both cars, taken boxes down from the attic, decided he would have the crew turn the space into a painting studio for Linda. He had climbed out Chloe's nursery window to empty the gutters, clawing out wet clumps of leaves and bird shit with his bare hands, hands gone blue and bloodless from the cold. When he'd wiped his cheek with his shirtsleeve, it came back damp. His whole face was wet. Even though he was crying, it was not unpleasant, like those times he'd taken mushrooms in high school and sat out in the nature preserve by Salt Point, tears streaming down his face when he felt the wave start to hit, his mouth filling with drool. On the roof he had leaned back on the shingles, considered the drop to the yard below. What had the calculation even been? Not high enough. He had not taken the pills again.

And how had it happened, the eventual neutering of his anger? He was too tired to knock things over. What had Sasha said, the last time they'd got in a fight? She'd been crying, on a trip about how he used to throw food at her when she didn't eat it. These things seemed so far away, and then eventually they got further away, and then nobody talked about them anymore.

When he brought the empty mugs down to the kitchen, Sasha was holding up a white package, a cardboard box opened in front of her.

"What are these?" she said.

"Where did you get that?"

"The box was on the counter. I just opened it, sorry."

He snatched it away. "Was it addressed to you?"

"Sorry," she said.

"You just do whatever you want?" He was aware that he was almost yelling.

"I said sorry." She looked scared in a way that made him angrier.

"You might as well have it," he said. "It doesn't matter anymore."

For Christmas he had bought everyone those DNA kits. Linda, too. A pretty good present, he thought. He had been proud—he'd got everyone a DNA kit and an AAA membership. Who could ever say he didn't think of his family?

Sam came into the kitchen, already dressed.

John slid a box toward him. "Here."

"What?"

"It's your Christmas present," he said. "You just spit into these tubes. It's all included. Send it off. It comes back and tells you exactly what your DNA is."

"Cool," Sam said, making a show of studying the package, turning it over in his hands.

"You know," Sasha said, "this is basically just giving your DNA to the police."

"But you guys can find your heritage," John said. "Find relatives. Learn about the family."

Sasha smirked. "This is how they found that man who killed everyone. The serial killer. Through some fourth cousin."

"They weren't cheap," he said, hearing his voice rise. Probably, he thought, his kids didn't even know his own father's name. Unbelievable. He took a breath. "I got one for everyone."

Sasha looked at him, looked at Sam. "Sorry," she said. "It's great. Thank you."

IN THE AFTERNOON, Chloe put on home movies. Sam had transferred all the tapes to DVDs as John and Linda's Christmas present the year before. Zero sat quivering beside

Chloe on the living room floor. The dog smelled, even from the doorway, faintly of urine. Chloe didn't seem to notice, nuzzling into his neck. She was eating a microwave burrito off a paper towel. It looked damp and unpleasant, oozing beans.

"Want to watch with me?" she said.

He was tired. The living room was warm, the heat on. It was fine to sit in the big chair, to close his eyes, listen to the voices. It was his voice. He opened his eyes. The camera was jerky, handheld, John walking it down an empty hallway. **Let's go say hi to everyone,** he said. **Let's go find them.**

It was a house they had not lived in for at least twenty years. What an odd house it had been. So many levels and nooks, big dark beams. A row of pine trees whose branches the kids used to grab through the car windows as he drove past, the snow that covered the bedroom skylight. How strange to see it again, conjured from nothing. Their old life. The camera caught his sneakers, the carpet, the flash of a tweed couch.

"Where is that?" Chloe asked.

"You were a baby. We only lived there a year or two."

It was hard to remember when it would have been exactly, but they lived in that house before Linda's father died, so it was probably '96 or '97. It looked like winter, and maybe it was the winter that bears kept breaking into the car, often enough that he had to leave it unlocked so that they wouldn't smash the windows. Sam liked seeing the muddy paw prints, though Sasha was deathly afraid of bears, wouldn't even come out to look at the tracks.

What else did he remember about the house—the stone fireplace, the collection of pig salt shakers, the cramped kitchen with its mustard-colored refrigerator that they packed with cubes of hot dogs, the freezer limping along, barely keeping the waffles solid. The girls had shared a room. Sam in that nook. They played Go Fish and War, they made houses of cards, they watched **Bedknobs and Broomsticks.** Linda's brother came over all the time. George was still married to his first wife, Christine—she was beautiful then, hair that curled up at the ends, breasts that were always half out of whatever shirt she was wearing. John pulled her onto his lap, and Linda slapped his shoulder, **Jo-ohn,** Christine wriggling off but only after a few minutes. George and Christine got divorced, how many years after that? Christine fat from antipsychotics and claiming that George had pushed her down the stairs.

"Look at Mom's hair," Chloe said. "It's so funny."

Linda was wearing glasses popular at that time, brown saucers that made her eyes a little goggled.

She waved the camera away. **John! Stop!** The video cut out. He closed his eyes again. He heard only static. Then:

Sam, sit down.

It's his birthday.

It was a nice present your grandpa got you.

The cake looks good.

Hold up how many fingers, how old?

It's a special puppet. Be very gentle with it.

What do you want to be? You want to be a doctor?

No.

Lawyer.

No.

President? Sam?

John, don't.

It wasn't me. It was this guy.

Don't touch the puppet. We'll be very careful with it. It's very expensive.

Sasha. The baby's sleeping. Don't touch.

Sasha stood in the doorway. "What are you guys watching?"

"It's so funny," Chloe said. "You should watch. You were so cute. Wait, let me put on the one of you. It's really cute."

The camera shook, pointed at the carpet. Then tilted up to Sasha in a nightgown, sitting on the bottom step of a staircase.

How old are you?

Five.

Who's that there?

Gecko.

Is that your Gecko? Is it Gecko? What are you doing?

Making a Flounder house.

Flounder?

Ariel and Flounder.

And who do you love? Do you love your daddy?

Yes.

Who do you love more, your daddy or your mommy? Do you love your daddy the most?

John glanced at Sasha, but she was gone.

SHE WAS IN THE KITCHEN, ripping paper towels off the roll, square by square, floating them on a puddle under the table. "Zero pissed again," she said. "Jesus," she said, the roll of paper towels now empty. She was almost sputtering. Her eyes were puffy and red. "Why doesn't anyone clean up the piss? It's disgusting. The dog pisses all over this house and no one even notices."

"Your mom loves that dog," John said.

Sasha nudged the paper towels along the floor with the toe of her boot. He guessed that she would not actually take the step of picking up the towels, actually cleaning up.

"Any news about your bag?"

Sasha shook her head. "There's this website to check, but it just says it's still in transit," she said. "I keep refreshing."

"I can take you to the mall if you want," he said.

"Okay. Yeah, thanks."

He stood for a moment too long, expecting—what? Nothing. She didn't pick up the paper towels.

SASHA WAS SILENT on the drive, thirty minutes up Highway 12. Not much traffic.

"You see they're still not done with the hotel?"

He'd been outbid on that job. Good thing, since it was all tied up with the city anyway, people writing letters to the editor, wanting traffic-impact reports.

Sasha kept checking her phone.

"Do you have a charger or something?" she said.

When he reached across her to get the one in the glove box, she flinched.

He forced himself not to say anything.

He should have let Linda drive her, or one of the kids. He put on the radio, already tuned to Linda's favorite station. It played Christmas music starting on Thanksgiving. Sam had told him that all radio was just programmed by computers now.

Yet in thy dark streets shineth
The everlasting light.

Hadn't one of the kids' classes done this song one year at a Christmas pageant? The kids dressed as angels in cut-up bedsheets, Linda making them halos out of tinsel.

Sasha pulled down the sleeves of Chloe's sweatshirt and put her phone, now plugged into the charger, on the console between them. The background of her phone, John saw, was a photo of a family on the deck of a ferry. A woman, a man, a kid. The woman, he realized after a moment, was Sasha. She was in a bright blue anorak—beaming, windswept. A young boy was sitting in her lap, and a man, Andrew, smiled with his arm around them both. The thought came clearly to John that they missed her. This man and his child. She was here and not there and they missed her. Why should that be so strange? The screen went blank.

She'd had a boyfriend in high school, or maybe it was Chloe's boyfriend, a rangy kid with a dark bowl cut, a sharp nose, raw, red nostrils. The boy had been nice enough, except that he'd eventually snapped—was it drugs? Or maybe he was schizophrenic, John didn't remember. His parents had called John and Linda once to see if the boy was staying with them. This was years after they'd broken up. The boy hadn't been staying with them, of course, and his mother told John over the phone how the boy had put a dead bird in the coffee machine, how he thought his family was trying to kill him. How he'd disappeared and they had no idea where he was or how to find him. John had felt bad for the boy's mother, embarrassed, even, by her unselfconscious grief, and glad for his own children: healthy, normal, off living their lives.

"Maybe you and Chloe should make persimmon cookies tonight?" he said.

"No one eats persimmon cookies. You don't even like them."

"I do like them," he said. He felt hurt. Though he couldn't remember what persimmons even tasted like. Astringent, maybe, soapy.

"All those persimmons are just going to rot if you don't," he said.

She didn't care. She didn't remember any of the good things. The night he'd woken them up, piled them into the back of his pickup with blankets, driven them to the reservoir, where they made a huge fire, where the kids sat on towels on the damp ground and ate burnt marshmallows off sticks. There was a photo from that night he used to keep on his desk, the three kids looking tired and happy and bundled in the bright, optimistic colors of that old clothing—and then how did that seem suddenly to mean nothing? Or the month all the kids had chicken pox and slept on sheets on the floor of his and Linda's bedroom, nude and dotted with calamine lotion, the bathtub drain clogged from their oatmeal baths. So many illnesses and broken bones and sprained wrists and cracked skulls.

They didn't care. As a girl, Sasha had

watched **The Wizard of Oz** so many times that the tape had snapped.

"Do you remember that?" he said. "How much you liked **The Wizard of Oz**?"

"What?" She looked irritated.

"You loved it. You watched it twenty-five times, more. It must have been more. You broke the tape."

She didn't say anything.

"It's true," he said.

"Sounds like Chloe."

"It was you."

"Pretty sure it was Chloe."

He tried to feel kindness toward her.

Even on Christmas Eve, the parking lot at the mall was full. He guessed he shouldn't be surprised by that anymore, people wanting to shop instead of being home with their families. It used to be shameful, like being on your phone when someone was talking to you, but then everyone did it and you were just supposed to accept that this was how life was.

"You can drop me off here," Sasha said, already opening her door. "This is good. You want to come back in, like, three hours or something? Meet back here?"

HE MIGHT AS WELL SWING by the office, just to check on things—no one was there, of course, no other cars in the office park, the heat turned off, but it was good to sit at his desk, turn on his computer, answer a few emails. He signed some checks. He liked the office when it was quiet. John drank room-temperature water, wobbling in a paper cone, from the water fountain. They should start ordering regular paper cups. Linda texted that the neighbor had called. Zero had got out somehow, made it a few houses before someone found him.

All ok now?

Fine, she texted back.

She'd said she'd wait until after Christmas to put Zero down, but now, with the pacemaker, who knew. The dog would probably outlive John. Another hour before he had to get Sasha. He found a granola bar in his drawer that crumbled when he opened the wrapper. He tipped the pieces into his mouth, chewed hard. Margaret was with her son in Chicago: photos of her grandson were on her bulletin board, a tin of tea sat on her desk along with the tube of hand cream she used assiduously. Before she left, Margaret had turned the calendar—a freebie from the hardware store—to January. He checked the time. He knew he was going to have to get up, sooner or later, but there was no reason to leave until he had to.

HE CIRCLED THE PARKING LOT once before he saw Sasha, leaning against a post, her eyes closed. She looked peaceful, untroubled, her hair tucked behind her ears, her hands in the pocket of Chloe's sweatshirt. If he remembered correctly, Sasha had not got into that college. She had never been a lucky girl. He rolled down the passenger-side window.

"Sasha."

Nothing.

"Sasha," he said, louder.

"I kept calling for you," he said, when she finally approached. "You didn't hear?"

"Sorry," she said, getting into the car.

"You didn't buy anything?"

For a moment, she looked confused.

"I didn't like anything," she said.

He started to pull away. It had rained at some point without his noticing; the streets were wet. Other drivers had turned on their headlights.

"Actually," Sasha said, "I didn't even look for clothes. I saw a movie."

"Oh?" he said. He couldn't tell if she was trying to elicit some specific response. He kept his face empty, his hands on the wheel. "Was it good?"

She told him what had happened in the movie.

"Sounds sad," he said.

"I guess," Sasha said. "Everyone said it was supposed to be good. But I thought it was dumb."

Sasha's phone chimed on the seat between them.

"But why would people want to go see a movie that makes them sad?" John said.

Sasha didn't answer him. She was busy typing, her face washed in the light from her screen. It had got dark so quickly. He turned on his own headlights. Her phone chimed again and Sasha smiled, a small, private smile.

"Is it okay if I call Andrew? Really quick. I'm just going to say good night," she said. "It's late there."

He nodded, keeping his eyes on the road.

"Hi, sorry," Sasha said, speaking low into her phone. "No," she said, "I'm in the car."

She laughed, softly, her voice dropping, her body relaxing into the seat, and at the stoplight John found himself tilting his head in her direction, straining to make out what she was saying, as if he might catch something in her words.

LOS ANGELES

IT WAS ONLY NOVEMBER BUT HOLIDAY decorations were already starting to creep into the store displays: cutouts of Santa wearing sunglasses, windows poxed with fake snow, as if cold was just another joke. It hadn't even rained since Alice moved here, the good weather holding. Back in her hometown, it was already grim and snowy, the sun setting behind her mother's house by five P.M. This new city seemed like a fine alternative, the ceaseless blue sky and bare arms, the days passing frictionless and lovely. Of course, in a few years, when the reservoirs were empty and the lawns turned brown, she'd realize that there was no such thing as unending sunshine.

The employee entrance was around the back of the store, down an alley. This was before the lawsuits, when the brand was still popular and opening new stores. They sold cheap, slutty clothes in primary colors, clothes invoking a low-level athleticism—tube socks, track shorts—as if sex was an alternative sport. Alice worked at a flagship store, which meant it was bigger and busier, on a high-visibility corner near the ocean. People tracked in sand and sometimes beach tar that the cleaners had to scrub off the floors at the end of the night.

Employees were only allowed to wear the brand's clothes, so Alice had gotten some for free when she started. Emptying the bag on her bed, she had been stirred by the pure abundance, but there was a caveat: her manager had picked them out, and everything was a little too tight, a size too small. The pants cut into her crotch and left red marks on her stomach in the exact outline of the zipper, the shirts creasing tight in her underarms. She left her pants undone on the drive to work, waiting until the last minute to suck in her stomach and button them up.

Inside, the store was bright white and shiny, a low-level hum in the background from the neon signs. It was like being inside a computer. She got there at ten A.M. but already the lights and the music conjured a perpetual afternoon. On every wall were blown-up photographs in grainy black-and-white of women in the famous underpants, girls with knobby knees making eye contact with the camera, covering their small breasts with their hands. All the models' hair looked a little greasy, their faces a little shiny. Alice supposed that was to make sex with them seem more likely.

Only young women worked the floor—the guys stayed in the back room, folding, unpacking and tagging shipments from the warehouse, managing stock. They had nothing to offer beyond their plain labor. It was the girls that management wanted out in front, girls who acted as shorthand to the entire brand. They patrolled their assigned quadrants, wedging fingers between hangers to make sure items were hung at an equal distance, kicking dropped shirts out from under the partitions, hiding a ruined leotard smeared with lipstick.

Before they put the clothes on the racks, they had to steam them, trying to reanimate the sheen of value. The first time Alice had opened a box of T-shirts from the warehouse, seeing the clothes there, all stuffed and flattened together in a cube without tags or prices, made their real worth suddenly clear—this was junk, all of it.

At her interview, Alice had brought a résumé, which she'd made some effort to print out at a copy store. She had also purchased a folder to transport the résumé intact, but no one ever asked to see it. John, the manager, had barely asked about her employment history. At the end of their five-minute conversation, he instructed her to stand against a blank wall and took her picture with a digital camera.

"If you could just smile a little," John said.

They sent the pictures to corporate for approval, Alice later discovered. If you made the cut, whoever did your interview got a two-hundred-dollar bonus.

Alice fell into an easy rhythm at her post. Feeding hanger after hanger onto the racks. Taking clothes from the hands of strangers, directing them to a fitting room that she had to open with a key on a lanyard around her wrist, the mildest of authorities. Her mind was glazing over, not unpleasantly. She'd get paid tomorrow, which was good—rent was due in a week, plus a payment on her loans. Her room was cheap, at least, though the apartment, shared with four housemates, was disgusting. Alice's room wasn't so bad only because there was nothing in it—her mattress still on the floor, though she'd lived there for three months.

The store was empty for a while, one of the strange lulls that followed no logical pattern, until a father came in, pulled by his teenage daughter. He hovered at a wary distance while his daughter snatched up garment after garment. She handed him a sweatshirt, and the man read the price aloud, looking to Alice like it was her fault.

"It's just a plain sweatshirt," he said.

The daughter was embarrassed, Alice could tell, and she smiled at the father, bland but also forgiving, trying to communicate the sense that some things in this world were intractable. It was true that the clothes were overpriced. Alice could never have bought them herself. And the daughter's expression was recognizable from her own adolescence, her mother's running commentary on the price of everything. The time they went to a restaurant for her brother's eighth-grade graduation, a restaurant with a menu illuminated with some kind of LED lights, and her mother couldn't help murmuring the prices aloud, trying to guess what the bill might be. Nothing could pass without being interrogated: had it been worth what it had cost?

When the father relented and bought two pairs of leggings, the sweatshirt, and a metallic dress, Alice understood he had only been pretending to be put off by the prices. The daughter had never considered the possibility that she might not get what she wanted, and whatever solidarity Alice felt with the father dissipated as she watched the numbers add up on the register, the man handing her his credit card without even waiting to hear the total.

—

OONA WORKED SATURDAYS, TOO. She was seventeen, only a little younger than Alice's brother, Sean. But Sean seemed like he was from a different species. He was ruddy-cheeked, his beard trimmed to a skinny strap along his chin. A strange mix of perversity—the background on his phone a big-titted porn star—and a real boyishness. He made quesadillas on the stove most nights, adored and replayed a song whose lyrics he happily chanted, "Build Me Up Buttercup," his face young and sweet.

Oona would eat Sean alive, Oona with her black chokers and lawyer parents, her private school where she played lacrosse and took a class in Islamic art. She was easy and confident, already well versed in her own beauty. It was strange how good-looking teenagers were these days, so much more attractive than the teenagers Alice and her friends had been. Somehow these new teenagers all knew how to groom their eyebrows. The pervs loved Oona—the men who came in alone, lured by the advertisements, the young women who worked the floor dressed in the promised leotards and skirts. The men lingered too long, performing a dramatic contemplation of purchasing a white T-shirt, carrying on loud phone calls. They wanted to be noticed.

The first time it seemed like one of those men had cornered Oona, Alice pulled her away for an imaginary task in the back. But Oona just laughed at Alice—she didn't mind the men, and they often bought armfuls of the clothes, Oona marching them to the cash register like a cheerful candy-striper. They got commission on everything.

Oona had been asked by corporate to shoot some ads, for which she would receive no money, only more free clothes. She really wanted to do it, she told Alice, but her mom wouldn't sign the release form. Oona wanted to be an actress. The sad fact of this city: the thousands of actresses with their thousands of efficiency apartments and teeth-whitening strips, the energy generated by thousands of treadmill hours and beach runs, energy dissipating into nothingness. Maybe Oona wanted to be an actress for the same reason Alice did: because other people told her she should be an actress. It was one of the traditional possibilities for a pretty girl, everyone urging the pretty girl not to waste her prettiness, to put it to good use. As if prettiness was a natural resource, a responsibility you had to see all the way through.

Acting classes were the only thing Alice's mother had agreed to help pay for. Maybe it was important to her mother to feel Alice was achieving, moving forward, and completing classes had the sheen of building blocks, tokens being collected, no matter if they had no visible use. Her mother sent a check every month, and sometimes there was a cartoon from the Sunday paper she'd torn out and enclosed, though never any note.

Alice's teacher was a former actor now in his well-preserved fifties. Tony was blond and tan and required a brand of personal devotion Alice found aggressive. The class was held in the rented room of a community center, with hardwood floors, folding chairs stacked against the wall. The students padded around in their socks, their feet giving off a humid, private smell. Tony set out different kinds of tea and the students studied the boxes, choosing one with great ceremony. Get Calm,

Nighty Night, Power Aid. They held their mugs with both hands, inhaling in an obvious way; everyone wanted to enjoy their tea more than anyone else enjoyed theirs. While they took turns acting out various scenes and engaging in various exercises, repeating nonsense back and forth, mirroring each other's improvised gestures, Tony watched from a folding chair and ate his lunch: stabbing at wet lettuce leaves in a plastic bowl, chasing an edamame with his fork.

Everyone trotted around the room in a loose pack, making intense eye contact, an exercise that Tony dubbed "Dog Park."

"Ian," Tony called from his chair, his voice weary. "We're not actually pretending to be dogs. Tongue back in your mouth."

Every morning in Alice's email, an inspirational quote from Tony popped up:

> DO OR DO NOT. THERE
> IS NO TRY. FRIENDS ARE GIFTS
> WE GIVE OURSELVES.

Alice had tried, multiple times, to get off the email list. Emailing the studio manager, and finally Tony himself, but still the quotes came. That morning's quote:

REACH FOR THE MOON.
IF YOU FALL SHORT,
YOU MAY LAND ON A STAR!

It seemed shameful that Alice recognized celebrities, but she did. A stutter in her glance, a second look—she could identify them almost right away as famous, even if she didn't know their names. There was some familiarity in the way their features were put together, a gravitational pull. Alice could identify even the C-list actors, their faces taking up space in her brain without any effort on her part.

A woman came into the store that afternoon who wasn't an actor, but was married to one: an actor who was very famous, beloved even though he was milk-faced and not attractive. The wife was plain, too. A jewelry designer. This fact came to Alice in the same sourceless way as the woman's name. She wore rings on most fingers, a silver chain with a slip of metal dangling between her breasts. Alice figured the jewelry was of her own design, and imagined this woman, this jewelry designer, driving in the afternoon sunshine, deciding to come into the store, the day just another asset available to her.

Alice moved toward the woman, even though she was technically in Oona's quadrant.

"Let me know if I can help you find anything," Alice said.

The woman looked up, her plain face searching Alice's. She seemed to understand that Alice recognized her, and that Alice's offer of help, already false, was doubly false. The woman said nothing. She just went back to idly flipping through the swimsuit separates. And Alice, still smiling, made a swift and unkind catalog of every unattractive thing about the woman—the dry skin around her nostrils, her weak chin, her sturdy legs in their expensive jeans.

ALICE ATE AN APPLE for lunch, tilting her face up to feel the thin sun on her forehead and cheeks. She couldn't see the ocean, but she could see where the buildings started to dissipate along the coast, the spindly tops of the palms that lined the boardwalk. The apple was okay, crisp and clean-fleshed, slightly sour. She threw the core into the hydrangea bushes below the deck. It was her whole lunch: there was something nice about the way her stomach would tighten around its own emptiness afterwards, how it made the day sharper.

Oona came out on the back porch for her break, smoking one of John's cigarettes. She had cadged one for Alice, too. Alice knew she was a little old to take this much pleasure in Oona, but she didn't care. There was an easy, mild rapport between them, a sense of resigned camaraderie, the shared limits of the job alleviating any larger concerns about where Alice's life was going. High school was probably the last time Alice had smoked cigarettes with any regularity. She didn't talk to any of those people anymore, beyond noting the engagement photos that surfaced online, the couple holding hands, walking on the railroad tracks during the golden hour. The men often wore vests, like old-time bartenders—when had this started? Worse: the photos of the couples cavorting by the ocean, or kissing in front of a stand of trees, photos name-dropping the natural world, the inane beauty of the sunset. Children followed soon after, babies curled like shrimp on fur rugs.

"It was the guy," Oona was telling her. "With the black hair."

Alice tried to remember if she'd noticed any particular man. None stood out.

He'd come in that afternoon, Oona said. Had tried to buy her underwear. Oona laughed when she saw Alice's face.

"It's hilarious," Oona said, dreamily combing her long bangs out of her eyes with her fingers. "You should look online, it's a whole thing."

"He asked you to email him or something?"

"Uh, no," Oona said. "More like, he said, 'I'll give you fifty bucks to go into the bathroom right now and take off your underwear and give them to me.' "

The upset that Alice expected to find in Oona's face wasn't there—not even a trace. If anything, she was giddy, and that's when Alice understood.

"You didn't do it?"

Oona smiled, darting a look at Alice, and Alice's stomach dropped with an odd mix of worry and jealousy, an uncertainty about who exactly had been tricked. Alice started to say something, then stopped. She moved a silver ring around her finger, the cigarette burning itself out.

"Why?" Alice said.

Oona laughed. "Come on, you've done these things. You know."

Alice settled back against the railing. "Aren't you worried he might do something weird? Follow you home or something?"

Oona seemed disappointed. "Oh, please," she said, and started doing a leg exercise, going briskly up on her toes. "I wish someone would stalk me."

ALICE'S MOTHER DIDN'T WANT to pay for acting classes anymore.

"But I'm getting better," Alice said to her mother over the phone.

Was she? She didn't know. Tony made them throw a ball back and forth as they said their lines. He made them walk around the room leading from their sternum, then from their pelvis. They lay on blankets from the closet that smelled thick with body odor, their eyes closed. Alice had finished Level One, and Level Two was more expensive but it met twice a week plus a once-monthly private session with Tony.

"I don't see how this class is different than the one you just took."

"It's more advanced," Alice said. "It's more intensive."

"Maybe it's okay to take a break for a while," her mother said. "See how much you really want this."

How to explain—if Alice wasn't taking a class, if she wasn't otherwise engaged, that meant her terrible job, her terrible apartment, suddenly carried more weight, maybe started to matter. The thought was too much to consider squarely.

"I'm pulling into the driveway," her mother said. "Miss you."

"You too."

There was only a moment when all the confused, thwarted love locked up her throat. And then the moment passed, and Alice was alone again on her bed. Better to hurtle along, to quickly occupy her brain with something else. She went to the kitchen, opening a bag of frozen berries that she ate with steady effort until her fingers were numb, until a chill had penetrated deeply into her stomach and she had to get up and put on her winter coat. She moved to catch the sunshine where it warmed the kitchen chair.

THERE WERE COUNTLESS ADS online, Oona had been right, and that night Alice lost an hour clicking through them, thinking how ludicrous people were. You pressed only slightly on the world and it showed its odd corners, revealed its dim and helpless desires. It seemed insane at first. And then, like other jokes, it became curiously tolerable the more she referred to it in her own mind, the uncomfortable edges softening into something innocuous.

The underwear was cotton and black and poorly made. Alice took them from work—easy enough to secret away a stack from the warehouse shipment before it got entered into inventory or had any tags on. John was supposed to check everyone's bags on the way out, the whole line of employees shuffling past him with their purses gaping, but he usually just waved them through. Like most things, it was frightening the first time and then became rote.

It didn't happen all that often, maybe twice a week. The meetings were always in public places: a chain coffee shop, the parking lot of a gym. There was a young guy who bragged about having some kind of security clearance and wrote to her from multiple email accounts. A fat hippie with tinted glasses who brought her a copy of his self-published novel. A man in his sixties who shorted Alice ten bucks. She didn't have any interaction beyond handing them the underwear, sealed in a Ziploc and then stuffed in a paper bag, like someone's forgotten lunch. A few of the men lingered, but no one ever pushed. It wasn't so bad. It was that time of life when any time something bad or strange or sordid happened, she could soothe herself with that thing people always said: it's just that time of life. When you thought of it that way, whatever mess she was in seemed already sanctioned.

OONA INVITED HER TO the beach on their free Sunday. One of her friends had a house on the water and was having a barbecue. When Alice pushed open the door, the party was already going—music on the speakers and liquor bottles on the table, a girl feeding orange after orange into a whirring juicer. The house was sunny and big, the ocean below segmented by the windows into mute squares of glitter.

She was uncomfortable until she caught sight of Oona, in a one-piece swimsuit and cutoffs. Oona grabbed her by the hand. "Come meet everyone," she said, and Alice felt a wave of goodwill for Oona, sweet Oona.

Porter lived in the house, the son of some producer, and was older than everyone else—maybe even older than Alice. It seemed like he and Oona were together, his arm slung around her bare shoulders, Oona burrowing happily into his side. He had thin hair and a pit bull with a pink collar. He bent down to let the dog lick him on the mouth; Alice saw their tongues touch briefly.

When Oona held up her phone to take a picture, the girl who was manning the juicer lifted her shirt to flash one small breast. Oona laughed at Alice's face.

"You're embarrassing Alice," she said to the girl. "Stop being such a slut."

"I'm fine," Alice said.

When Oona handed her a glass of the orange-juice drink, she finished it quickly, the acid brightening her mouth and her throat.

The ocean was too cold for swimming but the sun felt nice. Alice ate one greasy hamburger from the grill, some kind of fancy cheese on top that she scraped off and threw into an aloe plant. She stretched out on one of the towels from the house. Oona's towel was vacant—she was barefoot by the water, kicking in the frigid waves. Music drifted from the patio. Alice didn't see Porter until he flopped down on Oona's towel. He was balancing a pack of cigarettes on a plastic container of green olives, a beer in his other hand.

"Can I have a cigarette?" she said.

The pack he handed to her had a cartoon character on it, some writing in Spanish.

"Is it even legal to have cartoon characters on cigarettes?" she said, but Porter was already on his stomach, his face pressed into the towel. She palmed the pack back and forth, eyeing Porter's pale body. He wasn't even a little handsome.

Alice adjusted her bikini straps. They were digging into her shoulders, leaving marks. She surveyed the indifferent group back on the patio, Porter's unmoving body, and decided to take her top off. She chickened her arms behind herself and unhooked her bikini, hunching over so that it fell off her breasts into her lap. She was having fun, wasn't she? She folded the top into her bag as calmly as she could, sinking back onto the towel. The air and heat on her breasts were even and constant, and she let herself feel pleased and languid, happy with the picture she made.

Alice woke with Porter grinning at her.

"European-style, huh?" he said.

How long had he been watching her?

Porter offered her his beer. "I barely had any, if you want it. I can get another."

She shook her head.

He shrugged and took a long drink. Oona had walked far enough that Alice couldn't see her face, just her shape, the ocean foaming thin around her ankles. "I hate those one-pieces she wears," Porter said.

"She looks great."

"She's embarrassed about her tits," Porter said.

Alice gave him a sickly smile, and pushed her sunglasses back up her nose, crossing her arms over her chest in the least obvious way she could manage. They both turned at a commotion farther down the sand—some stranger had made his way to this private beach. The man seemed a little crazy, gray-haired, wearing a suit jacket. Probably homeless. Alice squinted: there was an iguana on his shoulder.

"What the fuck?" Porter said, laughing.

The man stopped one of Oona's friends, saying something she seemed to ignore, and then moved on to make his pitch to another girl, a blonde who looked unconvinced, her arms crossed.

Porter brushed sand from his palms. “I’m going inside.”

The man was now approaching Oona.

Alice looked at Porter but he was already gone.

The man was talking to Oona, his hands gesturing wildly. Alice didn’t know if she was supposed to do something, step in. But soon enough the man walked away from Oona and toward Alice. She hurried her bikini top back on.

“Want to take a picture?” the man asked. “One dollar.” The iguana was ridged and ancient-looking and when the man shook his shoulder in a practiced way, the iguana bobbed up and down, its jowls beating like a heart.

THE LAST TIME SHE ever did it, the man wanted to meet at four P.M. in the parking lot of the big grocery store in Alice’s neighborhood. It was a peculiar time of day, that sad hour when the dark seems to rise up from the ground but the sky is still bright and blue.

The shadows of the bushes against the houses were getting deeper and starting to merge with the shadows of the trees. She wore cotton shorts and a plain sweatshirt from work, not even bothering to look nice. Her eyes were a little pink from her contacts, a rosy wash on the whites that made it look like she'd been crying.

She walked the ten blocks to the parking lot. Even the cheapo apartment buildings were lovely at that hour, their faded colors subtle and European. She passed the nicer homes, catching slivers of their lush backyards through the slats of the high fences, the koi ponds swishy with fish. Some nights she walked around the neighborhood, near the humid rim of the reservoir. It was a pleasure to see inside those nighttime houses. Each one like a primer on being human, on what choices you might make. As if life might follow the course of your wishes. A piano lesson she had once watched, the repeated scales, a girl with a meaty braid down her back. The houses where TVs spooked the windows.

Alice checked her phone—she was a few minutes early. Other shoppers were pushing carts back into jangled place, the automatic doors sliding open and open. She lingered on a median in the lot, watching the cars. She checked her phone again. Her little brother had texted: **Miss u.** A smiley face. He had never left their home state, which made her obliquely sad.

When a tan sedan pulled into the lot, she could tell, by the way the car slowed, by the way the car bypassed an open space, that it was the man looking for her.

ALICE WAVED, FOOLISHLY, and the man pulled up next to her. The passenger window was down so she could see his face, though she still had to stoop to make eye contact. The man was bland-looking, wearing a fleece half-zip pullover and khakis. Like someone's husband, though Alice noticed no ring. He had signed his emails Mark but hadn't realized or maybe didn't care that his email address identified him as Brian.

The car looked immaculate until she caught sight of clothes in the backseat and a mail carton and a few empty soda cans tipped on their side. It occurred to her that perhaps this man lived in his car. He seemed impatient, no matter that they had both gotten here early. He sighed, performing his own inconvenience. She had a paper bag with the underwear inside the Ziploc.

"Should I just—" She started to hand the bag to him.

"Get in," he interrupted, reaching over to pop the passenger door. "Just for a second."

Alice hesitated but not as long as she should have. She ducked in, shutting the door behind her. Who would try to kidnap someone at four P.M.? In a busy parking lot? In the midst of all this unyielding sunshine?

"There," the man said when Alice was sitting beside him, like now he was satisfied. His hands landed briefly on the steering wheel, then hovered at his chest. He seemed afraid to look at her.

She tried to imagine how she would spin this story to Oona on Saturday. It was easy to predict—she would describe the man as older and uglier than he was, adopting a tone of incredulous contempt. She and Oona were used to telling each other stories like this, to dramatizing incidents so that everything took on an ironic, comical tone, their lives a series of encounters that happened to them but never really affected them, at least in the retelling, their personas unflappable and all-seeing. When she'd had sex with John that one time after work, she'd heard her future self narrating the whole thing to Oona—how his penis was thin and jumpy and how he couldn't come so he finally rolled out and worked his own dick with efficient, lonely habit. It had been bearable because it would become a story, something condensed and communicable. Even funny.

Alice put the paper bag on the console between herself and the man. He looked at the bag from the corner of his eye, a look that was maybe purposefully restrained, like he was proving he didn't care too much about its contents. No matter that he had found himself in a parking lot in the unforgiving clarity of midafternoon to buy someone's underwear.

The man took the bag but didn't, as she feared, open it in front of her. He tucked it in the side pocket of his door. When he turned back to her, she sensed his disgust—not for himself, but for her. She no longer served a purpose, and every moment she stayed in the car was just another moment that reminded him of his own weakness. It occurred to her that he might do some harm to her. Even here. She looked out the windshield at the cars beyond.

"Can I have the money?" she said, her voice going too high.

A look of pain fleeted across his face. He took out his wallet with great effort.

"We said sixty?"

"Seventy-five," she said, "that's what you said in the email. Seventy-five."

His hesitation allowed her to hate him, fully, to watch with cold eyes as he counted out the bills. Why hadn't he done this ahead of time? He probably wanted her to witness this, Mark or Brian or whoever he was, believing that he was shaming or punishing her by prolonging the encounter, making sure she fully experienced the transaction, bill by bill. When he had seventy-five dollars, he held the money in her direction, just out of reach so Alice had to make an effort to grab for it. He smiled, like she had confirmed something.

When she told Oona the story on Saturday, Alice would leave this part out: how, when she tried to open the car door, the door was locked.

How the man said, "Whoops," his voice swerving high, "whoops-a-daisy." He went to press the unlock button, but Alice was still grabbing at the door handle, frantic, her heart clanging in her chest.

"Relax," he said. "Stop pulling or it won't unlock."

Alice was certain, suddenly, that she was trapped, that great violence was coming to her. Who would feel bad for her? She had done this to herself.

"Just stop," the man said. "You're only making it worse."

MENLO PARK

HE'D BEEN THINKING HOW PRETTY the city looked from the plane window, spread out like a tablecloth, as if you could just shake off the crumbs and fold the whole city away. It had been a picturesque thought, Ben pleased with his tablecloth analogy, until the plane hit a pocket of air—the ground careened up at the window, the two vodka sodas he'd drunk lurching in his stomach. A drop of pure, blinkered terror—would he die staring at a seatback television playing reruns of **Frasier**?

They landed fine, in the end, his forehead only lightly pricked with sweat, a cocktail napkin shredded by his nervous hands. How quickly the possibility of annihilation was forgotten—the woman sitting next to Ben unbuckled her seatbelt, likely preparing to spring for the overhead bins the minute the seatbelt sign pinged off.

Ben left his seatbelt on. No rush, no need to find the baggage carousel: Ben never packed more than a carry-on as a matter of pride, and anyway, this was only a five-day trip. He'd gotten some work done on the flight, read over the newest draft from the ghost-writer. She seemed like a nice girl, not a bad writer, though the book was, of course, terrible. It was a memoir of Arthur's life, starting with his Kansas childhood, tracing the Stanford years, Menlo Park, the early days of the company, the explosion of outrageous fortune in the eighties. Arthur wanted to end the book with the board's takeover, a screed outlining his unfair ouster. Arthur felt he had been personally fucked by the universe, his downfall the result of prolonged and specific engineering by enemies, instead of the side effect of some light insider trading. Perhaps that's why Arthur had hired Ben to edit the book, some idea that they were both martyrs, victims, though Arthur was still a probable billionaire and Ben was, most certainly, not.

Arthur wanted the book to have the structure of a hero's journey, a request he kept repeating in his many lengthy emails, emails that lacked punctuation, emails that piled up in the night, emails that grew increasingly hysterical in tone, even without the use of exclamation points. Had Ben read Castaneda, Arthur wanted to know? Had Ben read Robert McKee? Did Ben know about the Dark Night of the Soul?

Ben buried the shredded napkin in the seat pocket, then settled back to turn his phone on. A bad feeling in his gut, nothing new. Even so, it was better knowing they were three hours behind New York, like he'd slipped out of time. Eleanor was not answering texts anymore, even if Ben said it was serious, made it sound like suicide was definitely a possibility. His last text to her—**Please?** She hadn't responded to him for months—since she heard they'd started the internal investigation.

There was a new way everyone was killing themselves lately, all these celebrities hanging themselves from doorknobs. Ben had his own theory about the appeal of the method, mostly that it was low-key and mellow and basically less embarrassing than other methods—from the articles he'd read, you pretty much got to sit down the whole time! Much more manageable than flinging yourself off a building or a bridge. Less dramatic. He called a suicide hotline once, after Eleanor had moved out but before his official dismissal. Ben had called mostly so he could later tell Eleanor he had—he'd immediately regretted it, the humiliation so great that he tried to hang up but found he could not, found himself robotically explaining the situation to a man who asked increasingly prurient questions about what exactly Ben had done and to whom.

There was a text from Arthur's assistant, confirming that a car would be waiting to pick him up (**Black Suzuki Kizashi, license plate PPF7780**). And at least Stephen's guy had texted him back, sent an address. Ben looked it up—it wasn't too far out of the way, barely a detour. Surely the driver would be fine with a quick stop. He relaxed.

The woman in the seat next to him sighed, her eyes fixed on the seatbelt sign. The instant the chime went off, she was up on her feet, pushing her way into the aisle, no matter the rows and rows that would have to drain before she could move forward.

THINGS HAD NOT BEEN GREAT, this last season. Enough months had passed that it might now, technically, count as more than a season, but it was comforting to imagine this mess cordoned off in a discrete unit of time, the benign kindergarten measurement of a season. Mostly he watched a tremendous amount of television, though he could no longer watch the show Eleanor produced, a show where celebrities discovered their genealogy. She always insisted, in her mild Midwestern accent, that it was dumb, but people seemed to enjoy it, delighted to watch an hour-long episode just to find out that Harry Connick Jr. was vaguely related to Buffalo Bill.

He was smoking again, taking too many drugs, though strictly pharmaceutical, strictly in pill form. This distinction seemed somehow adult. He blamed Stephen, blond, baby-faced Stephen, who showed up full of blistering tirades against the woman who'd replaced Ben, assurances that the office had fallen apart without him. Ideas for projects they could start together, a podcast, a Web series, a rich kid Stephen knew that he could hit up for funding, though Stephen was vague about when exactly the right time to approach this kid would be. "After the art fairs are over," he said, noncommittally.

Ben had always been great at talking to rich people. That had been a basic requirement of his old job, being able to charm and flatter the wealthy people whose houses they featured in the magazine, people who looked to him to offer their lives some tint of depth or culture, who donated money or joined the board in order to cement this feeling, this connection to him. Rich people made you feel like everything was possible, because for them, everything actually was. Spending too much time in their world, you start to believe in life's inherent goodness, start to feel safe, exempt, certain of your own luck. Ben let himself get lulled by the pure proximity of money—he had believed, even after everything, that he might still be saved. But those people had disappeared, too, in the end, except for the board member who gave Ben's name to Arthur, suggested he might freelance edit his memoirs, a last act of mercy. Or pity.

Ben was energized, in these moments, brainstorming with Stephen, the ashtray filling steadily from Stephen's cigarettes. As soon as Stephen left, Ben felt worse. He shouldn't smoke, shouldn't hang out with kids in their twenties. A buzzing in his head, a tight skull—certain refrains of songs looped and he said them aloud and smiled.

There was a night when he'd rushed to catch a train, late to meet a friend from the old days for a drink. The friend was ostensibly interviewing him for a job, but Ben knew it was a formality. Ben was, essentially, unhirable. Who knew for how long? Somebody must know these things, have some date in mind based on the relative severity of his misdeeds, but if so, no one was telling him.

He'd been breathless, late, taking the subway stairs two at a time. Pushing through the turnstile, he saw, to his immense relief, that a train was already in the station. The doors were closed—fuck!—but suddenly they opened with a pressurized exhale. Perfect. But then Ben saw he was the only person on the platform, and there was no one inside the train. The dread came all at once. Ben decided to take the next train. There, easy, the problem had been solved. But the train didn't leave, idling in the station with its doors open. He understood, in some oblique way, that he could not get on the train. That the train was waiting for him specifically. That to get on the train would mean passing from this world and into another. This was a ludicrous thought—there were many reasons why the train might be delayed—but it seemed to be there a long time, idling, and every moment that passed increased his panic. The train would not leave until he was inside. He was sure of it. The orange seats were lit brightly and he saw the back of the conductor's head and shoulders but could not see his face and somehow this was the most frightening thing of all.

"FLIGHT GOOD, ALL THAT?" the driver said.

"Yeah," Ben said, "thanks." He kept his bag with him in the backseat.

"We're lucky," the driver said, pulling into the lane that sluiced cars out of the airport. "Traffic shouldn't be so bad this time of day, going south."

"Actually," Ben said, leaning forward, "do you mind if we stop somewhere else first? I checked, and it's not really out of the way. It'll take a second."

The driver shrugged. He would not have a problem with a detour, or if he did, he wouldn't say so. He handed back his phone, nested in a giant phone case printed in camouflage. "Plug in the address?"

The directions took them to a neighborhood out toward the ocean—beige apartments with Spanish doorways, wooden decks that looked softened from sea air. The streets were wide compared to New York, though there were fewer people on the sidewalks, just students waiting for the train. They wore jackets and beanies, shivering in the fog. Two girls were zipped into one sweatshirt, hobbling like a strange beast on the platform, laughing.

"Should I park?" the driver said, pulling up to a stucco building.

"Nah. I'll only be a minute, seriously."

THE GUY WHO OPENED the apartment door seemed sleepy, trying to act businesslike though he was barefoot, his eyes at half-mast. He made a point of glancing behind Ben into the empty hallway.

"I thought you'd be a little later," the man said, pushing his feet into a pair of sandals by the door. "Come on in."

Inside the apartment, a girl sat on the couch, wearing a vintage dress cinched at the waist.

"This is Stephen's friend," the guy announced.

"Hi," the girl said, tucking her feet under the bell of her dress. Her hair was burgundy, a hair color Ben associated with 1993.

"And how do you know Stephen?" the man said, taking out a tackle box. He gestured for Ben to join him at the kitchen table.

"He's my assistant," Ben said. Or former

assistant, but who cared at this point? "He gave me your number."

"Nice guy, Stephen."

"Great guy."

This was the kind of non-talk meant to make them feel like this was a normal transaction. Like any other.

"Yeah, I should visit Stephen out there sometime," the guy said.

"You hate New York," the girl said from the couch. "You said it was"—here she paused for a moment, blinking—"terrible."

She glanced over at the table and shot Ben a disarming smile. Did she know about him? he wondered suddenly. Had she heard everything he'd allegedly done? He was being stupid. Of course she hadn't. When he left, the girl yawned on the couch, waved.

THE EXCHANGE WAS OVER, money had passed hands—success. Like a game, obstacles dodged and the reward reached, the chime of good things happening. Ben tried to swallow a pill in the stairwell, but he had to stop to cough, bracing himself against the wall. He tried to cough quietly, but the effort only made him cough harder until the pill finally broke apart in his throat.

"ALL GOOD?" THE DRIVER SAID, jerking to attention when Ben opened the door.

"A friend from New York," Ben said. "I just had to drop something off."

"New York's great," the driver said. "I been, oh, probably five times."

"Yeah," Ben said, "it's great."

He sat back in the seat, the car warm from the heater. He, too, had once thought New York was great. A great city. Ben's brother had visited him there. Only that one time. Poor Jude. Now living in an SRO in Long Beach, certain that his whole life was a television show, that he was being watched. His mother had once used a metal detector, waving it around Jude's head, trying to convince him it was a device that would turn off the voices. Weirdly, it had worked. Briefly, anyway.

Jude had visited him in New York before all that started, though probably there were clues. Even if there had been, Ben had been too consumed by his own life to notice anything amiss with his brother's. It was the year Ben had gotten promoted, a time when he was profiled by interviewers who ordered whole bottles of wine at expensed lunches, interviewers who called his old professors to hear specifics of his smarts, a time when he got emails of congratulations from people he had once idolized and had to mete out his attention at parties like it was a tangible resource, which he supposed it had actually been. He had not yet proposed to Eleanor but they both knew it would happen soon. It was a time of great fortune, Ben would think after, though that wasn't anything they said at the time, not aloud, or even thought to themselves—there was no reason to believe it might be temporary.

Ben didn't like to remember Jude's single visit. The silence that curdled between them. How Ben kept Eleanor away from Jude on purpose.

"Maybe we could go to a club," Jude had suggested one night, wearing a shirt that was brand new and buttoned tightly at the wrists and neck. It was Jude's first time on the East Coast. His brother, who had always been older, who had always known more. Who'd punched Ben in the stomach in front of his friends when he was twelve and tried to show him how to use a camcorder. Ben had not taken Jude to a club. Ben had not taken Jude to the Empire State Building. The ways he had been unkind—he didn't have a hard time remembering.

The car left the city. The hills were green, the fog dropping down through the canyons. The ground, when it was visible through all the green, was bright ocher.

"So, here on vacation?" the driver said.

"Just for work," Ben said, trying to forestall more conversation, though the driver didn't seem to track this effort.

"What kind of work?" he said.

"A book," Ben said. "Working on a book."

"Wow, you wrote a book?" The driver looked admiringly in the rearview.

How easily Ben was annoyed, his hackles up. "I'm only editing it. Someone else wrote it."

"So someone else does the writing?" Ben

couldn't see the driver's face but he could imagine it. "And you just help after? Cushy," the driver said.

He deserved the man's contempt. The driver didn't understand that Ben already felt bad, already felt cosmically punished. He wasn't supposed to think of these things, to go down tangents of imagining the situation turning out some other way. Maybe it was that Ben had been watching so much television lately, but reversals of fortune seemed somehow possible, the world infinitely malleable, people competing to bake cakes in the shape of flowers and dogs, winning thousands of dollars for it. The blood of Harry Connick Jr. and Buffalo Bill pumping the same strains of DNA. The miracle of nighttime falling in New York when here it was still light.

The landscape that churned past was so lovely that, for a moment, Ben forgot the good feeling was synthetic; the pill had started to work, a catch in his throat like pleasure at an unexpected gift—a sudden, surprised expansiveness, so he felt a surge of affection for the driver, so accommodating of his detour, affection for Arthur, who'd paid for Ben to be here, paid for this car to pick him up. Arthur, who believed Ben still had value.

What had it said in the latest draft of Arthur's book, whatever you dream you can achieve? **Whatever you dream.** It was so old fashioned, so Norman Vincent Peale. But Arthur was, what, nearing sixty? Ben's head was against the car window now, and he felt the car turning. When had they gotten off the freeway? The land was green and damp and mossy, like a Tolkien valley, one of the books his mother had read to him and Jude when they were boys. She had lit a candle while she read to them at night, a parenting tic that now seemed very peculiar. When he looked up, the driver was staring at him. The car was stopped.

"Brother?" the driver cleared his throat. "You all set?"

Ben sensed they had been stopped for a while. He tried to give the driver money for a tip but he wouldn't take it.

"It's included," the driver said, waving him away. Perhaps the look on the man's face was embarrassment.

—

THE NEW THING, ARTHUR TOLD BEN, was toad venom, much better than ayahuasca since it didn't last so long, and truly, he was a little scared of it because it was **fucking intense** but that was the exact reason to do it, didn't Ben agree? Did Ben know if you legally formed a religious group, you could avoid taxes and import certain ceremonial drugs without issue? Did Ben know that the U.S. had the power to turn off the Internet in another country?

"A whole country," Arthur said, hooting, "flip a switch and just total blackout. They should do it here, save us all from ourselves, but of course they won't."

Arthur was in a polo shirt and sweatpants. He had a rubbery face, like a sitcom star dialed up too many notches, and drank water at regular intervals from a metal water bottle clutched in his big paws. He showed Ben a photo of himself with the Pope, which seemed like a joke, in the same way it seemed like a joke when Arthur wrote Ben's name at the top of a blank piece of paper and underlined it twice. They sat in the living room of an old Victorian house on the property that Arthur had, for some reason, turned into a recording studio.

"Do you play music?" Ben said.

Arthur looked blandly at the microphones. "No," he said. "Maybe someday."

Arthur wanted to start off by going through the first chapter, page by page, essentially word by word. Surely Arthur must have somewhere else to be, his hours worth some unimaginable amount, but he seemed unhurried, ready to hunker down for the afternoon. He made Ben read each sentence aloud, Arthur's eyes closed, face straining to absorb each word.

"Okay," Arthur said, solemnly. "Very good."

Ben had never worked in this painstaking manner with anyone, but it was kind of nice, the way he had imagined books got edited when he was in high school. Certain things irked Arthur without reason—he wanted to use English spellings, didn't like Ben changing "girl" to "woman." Arthur stopped Ben in the middle of a sentence, got to his feet, then reached his arms toward the ceiling before slumping over, bent at the waist, swaying a little side to side.

"First you nod your head **yes,** then you shake your head **no,**" Arthur said, moving accordingly. "It's a good way to release the neck."

When Arthur righted himself, he was breathing hard, his face red.

Halfway through the first session, a man wandered in and sat down with Arthur and Ben. Arthur didn't introduce him. When the man looked at Ben, it was with the barest attention. He had rimless glasses and wore a Patagonia jacket, a jacket he didn't remove. He listened idly to Ben and Arthur discussing the chapter on Arthur dropping out of Stanford, making a show of his boredom.

"Can we get a little something," the man said, "a little snack, I don't know?"

Arthur sent a message on his phone and a different assistant arrived than the woman who had opened the gate for Ben. This girl was younger, European-seeming.

"Let's get Dave and Ben some knish," Arthur said, "that kind we had the other day?"

The girl laughed a little uncertainly. "Knish," she repeated. She had an accent.

"Knish," Dave repeated, imitating her, his pronunciation clumsy. The girl fell into a fit of giggles.

"K-nish," she said, "k-nish."

Arthur let his hand float at her hip for a brief second.

"Exactly."

BEN WASN'T IMAGINING IT—ARTHUR'S main assistant, Karen, was brusque with him, and he didn't know if it was because she had read the articles or tweets or whatever and was trying to forestall some imagined misdeed or if this was just her personality. She was responsible for ferrying him to and from the guesthouse where he was staying, on the far corner of the property. Normally, Ben would have been able to walk the distance from there to the Victorian where they were editing, but rains had washed out the road and she had to drive him the back way, her car sleek and spotless. He didn't care about cars but he knew it was an expensive one.

Karen was probably Ben's age, wore black leggings and running jackets, and had, actually, a nice body. He gathered she lived either on the property or very close by, and that she had worked for Arthur for at least a decade.

"How'd it go today?" she asked, and he said "Great" before she had finished the question.

A silence fell.

Ben was about to ask her whether she was from the area, but already Karen was back to talking about Arthur, the book project. They had created some self-publishing arm of Arthur's new business, hatched some plan to get this book into the hands of the young people, but Ben hadn't followed the relentless emails closely enough to weigh in.

"Just keep in mind we are wanting to get this book out by summer," Karen said. "He wants to distribute it at the music festivals, you know, though honestly we think we can finish it sooner. If you think that's possible?"

When Ben didn't say anything, she looked at him.

"Oh, yeah, for sure," he said. "That's totally possible."

She seemed pleased. And it was true, all

sorts of things seemed possible here. Whatever you dream you can achieve. That was, as Arthur was always saying, the main theme of his book. Ben said this line aloud to Karen, waiting for her mask to falter, for her to make some acknowledgment that she worked for a full lunatic, but her eyes just darted to his, her expression landing somewhere between confusion and boredom. She pulled up in front of the guest house, leaving the car running.

"Well thanks," he said. "For the ride."

Why did he linger in the car? Out of habit, or maybe boredom, he tried to hold Karen's gaze longer than necessary, smiling the old confident smile. A little game, harmless, seeing if she would play ball. He had been considered a charming man. Hadn't people said that?

He cocked his head a little, his smile clicking into a lower gear. And Karen smiled back, finally, her face going soft. She seemed, then, to get flustered, pushing her hair behind her ears, clearing her throat.

"Just text if you need anything," she said.

"I'll let you know what time Arthur wants to start in the morning."

THE GUESTHOUSE WAS LONELY. There was nothing on the walls except for a few black-and-white photos of peeling eucalyptus trees and a framed poster from a Big Brother and the Holding Company show at the Palace of Fine Arts. The windows looked out on greenness—the oaks, the neon hills, the steep edge of a canyon. There was an espresso machine and the refrigerator was empty except for a canister of coffee beans and a box of baking soda. The Internet was shockingly fast, the cell reception impeccable—Ben wished it wasn't, so he could imagine Eleanor had called him back and he had just missed it.

ARTHUR WANTED HIS BOOK to have a stand-alone chapter on human potential. Arthur wanted an appendix of his favorite quotations by great thinkers. Arthur wanted his morning routine reproduced on the flaps of the book jacket. Arthur's phone background was a list of his monthly goals. He skipped breakfast and ate only a green vegetable slurry for lunch so he could eat sickening amounts of food for dinner. Arthur did not drink alcohol. Arthur believed yogurt cured heartburn. When Ben bored him, his eyes pinballed in search of other information, though he would leave a smile on his face, inert. When he was thinking, he stood up and bounced from foot to foot. If Ben went to the bathroom, usually to take a pill with a slug of warm water scooped with his hand directly from the faucet, he returned to find Arthur in Child's Pose on the carpet. "Then we transition into Corpse Pose," Arthur said, sprawling on his back, eyes closed. One general life trick, Arthur told Ben in a conspiratorial tone, was to listen to audiobooks at 1.5 speed, so you got through them faster.

Arthur was concerned, he told Ben, that the ghostwriter's chapters were slack.

"In terms of momentum," Arthur said, stabbing at a page, "**forward motion.** Don't you think? Have you read Stephen King's book on writing?"

Ben agreed, yes, definitely, the pages were reading a little limp. Arthur relaxed, drank a glug of water.

"Maybe you should rewrite all this," Arthur said, waving his hand over the pile of pages. "Hmm? What do you think of that?"

Ben demurred. "I'm just here to edit," he said, though Ben had always privately believed he would be a good writer. Maybe great.

When they fell into what Arthur announced was "an energetic rut," Arthur took Ben for a drive in his car along the back roads, deep in the redwoods. His car was immaculate, the air tight with the off-gassings of the leather seats. Arthur turned on the stereo, blasting a song from fifty years ago, the sound system perfectly calibrated to soak them both in the audio.

"You like this guy?" Arthur said, almost shouting, gesturing at the speakers.

Ben nodded. "Sure."

"He lived around here in the sixties.

Wrote this very song while he was living on his ranch, basically next door to my spot," Arthur said. "Did you know that?"

Ben shook his head.

"Can you believe it? A twenty-year-old kid writing a song like this?" Arthur turned the music up. "He crashed right around here. Blammo, right into a redwood. You wanna go see? See where the great man died? Let's see, I marked the coordinates. Exact coordinates! It should be saved."

Arthur messed with the screen on the car's dashboard, a GPS map shifting and reloading, changing perspectives, the red arrow coursing along the on-screen streets like a video game avatar. Occasionally a woman's voice would cut through the music, telling Arthur to take a left in four hundred feet, or stay right at the next fork. The volume level on the speakers was turned up so high that they seemed to be inside the woman's mouth.

They looked, according to the map, to have almost reached the destination when Arthur missed a turn. The GPS instructions had been very clear but he'd still sailed past, causing the GPS to beep in alarm. Arthur was suddenly panicked, eyes jerking between the screen and the road. The car lurched, then accelerated.

"You let me miss the turn," Arthur shouted at Ben with genuine anger. In a way, it felt nice to have someone be mad to his face. Before Ben could respond, the woman's voice filled the car, crisp, relentless:

"Calculating, calculating."

THREE DAYS HERE, and they'd only edited up to the fourth chapter. Ben printed out the fifth chapter and reread it at the kitchen table of the guesthouse, drinking a glass of warm white wine from the case he'd found in the pantry. According to the label, the wine was biodynamic. It was the color of marmalade, full of sediment that coated his teeth.

Was it just the wine mixed with half a pill, or was this fifth chapter genuinely moving? He took a drink, flipped the page. Arthur had never been on an airplane until flying to Stanford from Kansas at age seventeen. It was touching to imagine: young Arthur exiting the plane, the warm California wind greeting him off the tarmac. Sweet. He had started, actually, to like Arthur.

Maybe, since they were so far behind, Arthur would ask Ben to stay on longer. Or maybe, when this project was over, Arthur would hire him full-time, maybe there was some kind of position available. Or maybe Ben would actually rewrite the book. Then use the money he made to write his own. It was nice in the guesthouse, deep in the blue shadows of all these redwoods. You could make a life up here, only descending the mountain once in a while, for necessities.

He opened a new email before he could think too much about it.

How to phrase it in a way that Arthur would find convincing—maybe make a point of how similar they were, he and Arthur. Men who persevered. Add a dash of that muddy Beat mysticism Arthur was so horny for.

. . . as you taught me, what you dream you can achieve, and I truly believe that I am the best person to write this book. Jack Kerouac said, "The only people for me are the mad ones, mad to live, mad to die, people who burn, burn, burn like

roman candles"—he'd look up the exact quote before he sent it—**When I met you, I recognized you, instantly, as one of these "mad ones." A secret sharer. And that's only one of the reasons I feel I have a mandate to tell your story.**

Before he realized it, the email was four paragraphs long. It was the longest piece of writing he'd done in months. He copied and pasted the right quote—he hadn't remembered that last part, the line about the roman candles exploding like spiders—and skimmed the email twice.

Good, he thought. Pretty good. He pressed send.

He brushed his teeth, barely, and was taking out his contacts in the bright marble bathroom, his mind wandering, when he suddenly realized he'd lost one of his contacts, that it must have slipped behind his eyeball. He swiped his fingers at his eye—nothing. There in the contact case on the counter was one single contact, a ghostly circle floating in the solution. One contact already in the case, the other—where, slipping around his skull? His heart was beating fast. Hadn't he once read a news story where this had happened to someone? Hadn't the woman eventually gone blind? He pulled out his right eyelid, pushing his face close to the mirror, blinking hard. Already his eye was tearing up, and when he tried again to grasp for the lens, it stung. Had he scratched himself somehow? He sat on the cold floor. He was crying but only from the right eye. He touched the wetness, convinced it would be blood.

KAREN SOUNDED SUSPICIOUS ON the phone, like this was some ruse he'd devised to get her to the guesthouse late at night. But when he answered the door, weeping from one eye, Karen seemed to soften. She led him to a chair in the kitchen under the bright overhead light, where he sat with his head tilted back. He felt very young suddenly, his throat exposed, wearing a T-shirt, his feet bare. He was vaguely aware that the kitchen was dirty, that there was an empty bottle of wine in the sink and another bottle, half full, uncorked and left out on the counter. She was near to his face, holding open his eyelid with two fingers. He could smell her breath: gamy, savory, she must have just eaten dinner. He wondered, idly, if she had a partner, or if she'd eaten alone. Her hair was down her shoulders, a little wet from a shower.

"I don't see anything," Karen said. "Now I'm just going to use the flashlight on my phone," she said, talking very slowly. "I'm sure we'll get it."

His left eye was closed tightly, Karen almost straddling him. His right eye shuddered in the wash of the flashlight, his eyeball rolling around.

"I don't want to hurt you," she said.

"You don't see it? Can you feel it?"

He felt her finger almost touch his eyeball, then spring back. "Sorry, I can't do this," she said. "I'm just worried I'm going to scratch you."

Ben sat with both his eyes closed, his right eye feeling swollen, enlarged in its socket. It was better to keep both eyes shut, to know Karen was here at the table.

"Is there a hospital or something?" he said, his eyes still closed. "I just don't want it to get bad."

"Maybe you'll just blink it out during the night? Like, it'll come out while you sleep?"

"Maybe." When he opened just his left eye, he saw Karen was sitting too close, her chin resting on a propped elbow.

"Hi," she said, smiling in a queer way.

It took him a moment before he realized: the energy in the room was familiar from what he thought of as the old days. When women seemed to hold his gaze meaningfully and punctuate their anecdotes with little touches of his arm, and that's what he was shocked no one had ever talked about, how many of the women had pursued him, called him. Even Eleanor had gotten his email from a friend and written him with a question about a movie he had introduced at a screening the week prior.

"Does it hurt very badly?" Karen said, making a gesture like she was about to touch his face.

Ben was on edge now, not only because of the lens he was sure was hardening into shards that might puncture his optical nerve, but this sense of Karen leaning closer. He had forgotten what came next—he was meant to lean in, too, to keep her gaze, but his eye hurt too badly and he worried suddenly that Eleanor would find out Karen was here, here in his house. Of course it didn't matter, of course Eleanor no longer cared. She was supposedly staying with her mother in Key West. Why? She was scared of the ocean. On their honeymoon, she hadn't left the towel, had gotten sunburned reading through the diaries of John Cheever, a sunburn so bad she couldn't sleep or stand to be touched.

Ben got to his feet.

"I'm sure it's fine," he said, "really."

"But if you're in pain?" Karen stood up. Through his squinted eye he saw that she was not wearing a bra. She was very attractive, he thought, but the thought just hovered, inert, unattached to anything. Is this what they had wanted, what everyone had wanted? For him to have these neutered, benign thoughts about women, thoughts that did not immediately translate into action? It wasn't the worst thing.

"Sorry," Ben said, "to have bothered you."

"I should let you get some sleep," Karen said.

She went to the sink, made a show of rinsing the empty bottle, putting it in the recycling. He could just wrap this night up. Both of them could go to bed. But he didn't move. Karen could speak to Arthur for him. That wasn't a bad idea, was it? Karen talking up Ben. Telling Arthur Ben should take over the writing of the book. He would never have to go back to New York.

"Do you want a glass of wine or something?" he said, clearing his throat. "I feel bad. Making you come over for this."

She considered, for a moment, a question in her face that he couldn't quite parse.

"Why not?" She poured herself a glass of the open wine and refilled his glass. She put the bottle in the fridge. He sat down so he could keep both of his eyes closed. Concentrate on the task at hand.

"I've really liked working with Arthur," he began.

"He's actually a really good boss." Karen's voice floated through the buzzy darkness. "Arthur."

"Mm. I know he's not that happy with the book. Right now, I mean. This last draft."

He could hear that Karen had sat down, too.

"I'm not sleeping with him," she said, and laughed. "I mean, just so you know. If that's what you're worried about." She had misinterpreted something in his tone. Had he lost it, the ability to control a conversation, stand back and watch it take its intended shape?

"Of course not," he said. The idea had honestly not occurred to him. "You're too good for Arthur." He smiled the old smile. When he opened one eye, to gauge the smile's effect, Karen was close.

"You're sweet," Karen said, laughing again.

Which of them leaned forward first?

Ben used to be so in control, in situations like this, that time would slow down to an almost comically chewy speed, every centimeter of movement observed, every breath noted. Like how the spy in those movies had been able to take in every detail of the crowded train station—the ticking clock, the woman pushing the baby carriage, the train arriving on track four, the train leaving on track five —digesting all the variables, calculating the correct path of action in the split second before he shot the villain in the head.

But something had happened. Ben was disoriented, no longer had the ability to locate himself, much less anyone else. Everything was murky, his own thoughts dim, Karen's thoughts unimaginable. They were kissing. He was kissing her back, or maybe she was kissing him back. It was dizzying, how little he knew.

He pulled away. "Sorry."

Karen looked stricken. He should have waited to bring up Arthur some other time, bring up the job—because when he did, blurting it out in the silence after he apologized, her face darkened. It took a second for him to read her expression. She was angry. It startled him how angry she looked. His hand reflexively went up to cover his right eye, maybe to remind her that he was actually hurt, that she should feel sorry for him, but she rolled her own eyes and stood up.

She stared at him, filled with—what? Hatred, pity?

"Really?" she said.

He could tell she wanted some response from him, needed it, but he couldn't muster anything. Sadness hovered in the room. Arthur wouldn't have a job for him. Eleanor wasn't coming home. Karen banged the door shut, flouncing out into the darkness.

Ben's eye ached but it wasn't unbearable. His felt his heart beat in his eye socket.

Chapter 5 was stacked on the table. At least Arthur got to tell his story. Or have a ghostwriter tell his story. Put it all in one place, link it together, so whatever had happened in his life seemed to beget the next thing that happened, step after step in one long and glorious ascension. It wasn't fair. Eleanor had never even let Ben try to explain himself, while Arthur got ninety thousand words to lay it all out. Arthur's many failures—the SEC fines, stepping down from his own company, the agreement that Arthur would never hold an executive position in any business again. Somehow the book had taken this raw evidence and massaged it into the shape of something even better, a tale of success and perseverance. The ghostwriter was, actually, fucking great at her job.

It occurred to Ben, looking at the stack

of chapter pages, that he could see the pages clearly, could see everything from his left eye clearly, which meant he must have a contact lens in after all. The lens he'd seen in the contact case was from his right eye. The other was in his left. Nothing was lost, all had been accounted for. He laughed, giddy with his own stupidity. An hour of clawing at an empty eye! All this useless terror!

Ben had the impulse to text Karen, tell her everything was fine, that it had just been a false alarm. It was funny, wasn't it? A funny story? How scared he'd been, over nothing? So certain he was in danger!

But he didn't text her. And when he did hear from Karen, it was a text—curt, arriving at seven A.M. the next morning—informing him that Arthur no longer required his services, though Ben would be paid the outstanding amount of his fee. A driver would be at the guesthouse in an hour to take Ben to the airport, to take him back the way he'd come.

Ben was about to formulate a response, his throat already starting to close, his forehead sweating, when three dots appeared on-screen, Karen still texting—saying what? Explaining? Was someone, finally, about to apologize to him?

He waited. Then her text arrived:

> **BLACK BMW X3,**
> **LICENSE PLATE FMX2217**

SON OF FRIEDMAN

THE LIGHT IN THE RESTAURANT WAS golden light, heavy light—an outdated sort of light, honestly, popular in the nineties but now a remnant of a kind of gaudy, old-school pleasure it was no longer fashionable to enjoy. It had been five years, maybe more, since George had been to this place. It was true that the food was not very good. Big steaks, creamed vegetables, drizzles of raspberry coulis over everything, all the food you ate back then because caring about what you ate wasn't yet part of having money. Still, he liked the fleshy Mayan shrimp on ice, the gratifying emptiness when the meat popped from the socket. He wiped his fingers, tight from lemon juice and shrimp, on the napkin in his lap.

"More bread?" Kenny asked.

It didn't seem possible that Kenny still worked here, all these years later, but here he was. Soft-faced Kenny, sweet, with a slight overbite. He had been a playwright, if George remembered. He used to give Kenny extra tickets to whatever show he was producing or whatever screening, and the next time he saw him Kenny would give him feedback with studied, professional effort. Maybe he had hoped George might hire him for something. In one swift motion, Kenny proffered a box of rolls and hovered a pair of tongs over the selection.

"Whole wheat," George said. Better for you, he thought. "Or actually," he said, "just the plain."

"Sure thing."

William was now twenty minutes late. There was work George could do—a producer had sent him a link to some David Hume thing. What were you even supposed to call things like that—a treaty, a treatise? The thought of squinting at the screen depressed him. And, really, who thought something like that was adaptable, some tedious old-timey screed? People were hot for it, though, death. The Hume had been mentioned in one of these columns everyone was reading, part of a series by this scientist who was terminally ill. Multiple people forwarded him links every week:

"in tears right now"

"Hold your loved ones tight!"

George read one of the essays on the **Times** website, trying hard to summon the reality of his own demise. He was seventy-one, with a fake knee and a hip due for replacement; it shouldn't be difficult. The scientist wrote about hovering above his own life, seeing each part of it like a dream from which he would soon wake. This is just a dream, George told himself. It's all vapor. George had squeezed out nothing but a vague awareness of the grammatical errors in the text. Some lines of inquiry were not ultimately helpful. He was on his second martini. Another thing that used to be stylish and had fallen out of favor. The antiseptic chill, the bracing rinse—why had he ever stopped drinking them?

—

HE FIRST SAW WILLIAM in the mirror behind the bar, pushing through the door in a watch cap and an overcoat, those famous eyebrows bristling. George's heart was pounding, a jolt from the cold alcohol. He turned to wave William over, and, in the moment before William saw him, something in the set of his face gave George the sudden intimation that the night would not go the way he had hoped.

The coat girl made a fuss over William—the host, too, clapping him on the back—and by the time he finally made his way to the bar the whole restaurant seemed aware of his presence, a certain background thrum of people whispering, maybe trying to take a picture with a phone held low, darting a look at him, then staring off into the middle distance. Even so, William moved through the room easily, without self-consciousness. Or at least he was adept at appearing that way.

"My friend," he said. George had to lean awkwardly on his stool to return the hug.

"I walked in and thought, Who's that old

guy waving at me at the bar?" William said. "And then it was you. And we were both old."

William settled on the stool next to him. It had been a little less than a decade, probably, since they'd seen each other on purpose.

"You mind if we just eat here?" George said. "Or I can ask about a table."

"Not at all. Is Benji not coming?"

George hadn't even considered asking his son to join them. Maybe that was strange. "He's with his girlfriend. They wanted to do their own thing."

"Getting ready for his big night," William said. "Good for him."

"I know he appreciates this. Benji. We both do."

"Of course."

William was Benji's godfather. When George's first wife, Patricia, had given birth, William and Grace were their first visitors in the hospital. William took Benji to Dodgers games, threw quarters in the pool at the Brentwood house and let Benji dive for them. That was right after George's third movie, the second he'd done with William. They took trips up to Ojai, out to Catalina for the day, the wives went shopping for Oscars dresses together. George had a first-look deal with Paramount, a steady stream of projects in development. It was almost embarrassing how fervently George had believed that everything would continue to get better and better, life a steady accrual of successes, of moments becoming only more vivid and more pleasurable. Then George had got divorced and moved to New York, after which his career slowed down, gradually and then all at once. Viacom bought Paramount. William's phone numbers changed faster than George could track them. After a couple of years, William didn't even call the boy on his birthday anymore. It rankled George, but Benji didn't care. And William was here, anyway, had come out to Benji's little movie and would get his photo taken standing next to Benji, maybe say some nice things about it, and that wasn't nothing.

Kenny filled a glass of water and set it in front of William. "Can I get you a drink to start?"

William was already chugging the water and shook his head, still swallowing. "Just water is fine for me."

Kenny receded, ever the professional, though George sensed his excitement, a new degree of alertness.

"The martinis here are excellent."

"Grace had me cut out alcohol," William said. "We're actually both doing it. For about six months, and, I have to say, it was hard but it's been great."

Incredible, when you thought about it, someone like William staying with the same woman all these years, but Grace was a good one. The summer they were shooting in Turin she had hosted parties at their big rented house, turned out heroic dinners for forty people, bringing platters of fish to the table in a long dress and bare feet, and who wouldn't want to stay married to someone like that? George had been divorced twice. Never again, though his girlfriend was pressuring him to let her move in, her and her daughter. It wasn't enough for her that he paid for her fillers, rented an apartment for her, paid for her daughter's dyslexia tutor. Just the thought of them made him weary.

"How is Grace?" George asked.

"Good," William said, scanning the menu.

“You know her, always busy. She started this foundation that pays college tuition for kids on reservations, so she’s always flying out to Utah or some such. She gives these kids her cell number, so some sixteen-year-old calls her in tears during dinner and she’s off dealing with that.”

George had been counting on a certain loose camaraderie, nostalgia tipping slightly toward sloppiness. William not drinking made things harder. George tried to sip his martini more slowly. He could probably order another and pretend it was only his second.

“And how is Lena?”

“She’s busy, too. Just got married, actually, to a guy from business school,” William said. “A big British guy. I like him.”

“I’m glad to hear it.”

The last time George had seen Lena, she was still in braces, hanging around the set doing homework, asking the makeup girls to do her eyeliner. He remembered because at the same time he was getting calls from Patricia, needing money for some new clinic for Benji, some program out in the desert or in the Alaskan wilderness, remote enough that the kids couldn't get their pills. The places all cost thousands of dollars, all solved nothing. All staffed by unattractive people in their late twenties, professional narcs with bad skin and waterproof sandals. Didn't they have better things to do? How sweet had Lena seemed to him: polite, her hair combed, mouthing the words silently as she read **White Fang** for English class.

"Grace is just happy they're moving to Los Angeles," William said. "She wants us to be those very involved grandparents." He laughed. "She's got the energy for it. I don't think Lena's guy knows what he signed up for."

THEY BOTH ORDERED THE HALIBUT, old men avoiding red meat, and the square of fish arrived in the center of an overly large plate, scattered with vegetables, some kind of micro-sprout. George took one bite and wished the food were better. But at least the movie theater was right next to the restaurant.

"We're good on time?" William asked.

"We're fine." They had another half hour before they should head over.

"Are you excited?"

George didn't follow.

"The movie," William said.

"The movie." George tried to indicate—by his expression, his tone of voice—some shared trepidation, an acknowledgment that he understood the movie would be bad, that they didn't have to pretend. William's expression didn't falter, arranged with pleasant blandness.

"Have you seen it yet?" William said.

"No, actually. Tonight's the night."

This seemed to surprise William. "You'd think he'd want the old man's expertise, huh?"

Had that word, "expertise," been tinted with sarcasm? No, George was being paranoid. What did William use to tell people? That George had a magic brain. What's going on in that magic brain, he'd ask, What's next?

"I think my opinion," George said, "is exactly what Benji didn't want."

Benji had wanted money, anyway. George hadn't exactly worked in a while, was living off reserves and the sale of the loft. He hadn't planned to give Benji anything until he found out that Benji had set up a GoFundMe page. The website featured slo-mo footage, set, inexplicably, to "Clair de Lune," of Benji and his burnout roommate walking on the campus of Santa Monica City College, hands in the pockets of their fleeces. A voice-over by Benji made somber assurances that this movie would be unlike any other, would explore a new kind of filmmaking. It was a movie about love, he said, a history of love, a documentary diving deep on "the thing that drives us all in every way."

The thought that Benji had emailed people—George's colleagues, family, friends—a request for ten thousand dollars to film his little movie horrified George.

"Don't be an asshole," Patricia had said. At least Benji was showing initiative, she said, interest in something. Benji was getting credits, would maybe even scrape together his degree, and that in and of itself was encouraging. Benji had quit so many things by that point: internships George had wrangled for him, jobs he stopped showing up to after two weeks. Some rip-off cooking school upstate—Benji had left early with a self-diagnosis of Lyme disease.

But why, George asked, couldn't he show interest in something, anything else?

He's trying to connect with you, Patricia told him. "Your son," she said, "looks up to you."

He could hear her husband say something in the background. The anesthesiologist.

"What's that?" George said. He felt, at times, almost insane. "Does Dan have some advice?"

"Call your son," she said, then hung up.

The plan was that Benji would pay George back. With interest. Unlikely.

"I think it's great," William said. "Benji wants to do this thing on his own. Not ride his dad's coattails."

That was laughable.

"It's a lot to live up to," William went on. "Having a father like you."

That pleased George. And by then the martinis had accrued, and his anxiety had quieted a little. They had had good times, he and William. This was his friend. He felt himself relax.

"I'd rather he was, I don't know, a dentist," George said. "A garbageman."

"You know," William said, wiping his mouth. "Garbagemen actually get paid really well. It's this coveted job. I heard a radio show about it."

Benji had been a nervous child. How to describe the revulsion George sometimes felt when Benji visited him for two weeks after Christmas—always sick, always getting injured. The time when he was nine or so, and tried to show George and his girlfriend—it was Monica then—some kind of cartwheel in the kitchen of the SoHo place. Benji crashed into the edge of the island, his lip split open and his mouth wet with blood. He was stunned, for a moment, then inconsolable. He seemed to take the injury as a personal betrayal by George. George had called down to the doorman to get a car, Benji on Monica's lap with a bath towel pressed against his face. Monica wiped Benji's cheek, looking at George with resignation and pity. Like this is just what George did: caused pain he was too inept to deal with. She had stayed with him through awards season, if he remembered correctly, then left him to move in with a woman.

"What are you up to these days?" George said. "Anything on the horizon?"

"One of these silly movies," William said. "You know. Two old guys on a road trip. I never thought I'd do these things. I thought I'd retire. But they drag you back, right?"

William had finished only half his halibut; George saw him scan for Kenny.

"You should see the set," William said. "It's so efficient, basically on autopilot. Nothing like we used to do—all the nuttiness, the yakking, herding the clowns. They got this stuff nailed down now. I'm in and out in two weeks. Grace is happy that I'm staying busy. I get a free haircut. Win-win."

"Staying busy is good," George said. He noticed that he was tapping his foot and made himself stop. "Actually," he said, "that's related to what I wanted to ask you—"

"I'm sorry," a woman said, hovering by William's stool. How had George not noticed her creeping up? She was a younger woman, maybe in her early thirties, bundled in a winter coat, her cheeks ruddy, darting quick looks back at the friend who hovered behind her. They looked like they should be scrubbing laundry a hundred years ago. The woman started laughing, breathless.

"I never do this," the woman said, her accent maybe Australian. "Really, I just wanted to say hi, and I'm just a big fan of your work."

William put down his fork and knife with easy patience. Why did his performative kindness make George suddenly annoyed?

"Well hello there," he said. "I'm so happy to meet you. What's your name?"

The woman looked at her friend again, both of them giggling now.

"Sarah," she said. "And Mae." Mae was readying her phone. "Do you mind if we take a picture?"

"It's so nice to meet you, Sarah, Mae," William said, shaking Sarah's hand, the other hand on her shoulder, and somehow, without them being aware of it, he maneuvered both women back a few steps. "I don't actually take photos these days, I hope you understand, but thank you again for coming by and saying hello." He smiled, warmly but with finality. "And you two have a great night."

William turned back to George. Behind him, the girls were blinkered, dazed; they stood a moment too long before shuffling backward, then finally speed-walking toward the door, chattering to each other in low excited tones.

"Sorry," William said. "Sorry. You gotta be nice nowadays or they put you online and say how mean you are."

"Right." George was flustered by the interruption. He had lost the thread. "What I did want to run past you, what I did think you'd like—" He felt the scratch of some bit of food come loose from his molars, a piece of fish bone that lodged itself in the soft skin in the back of his throat. He coughed once, hard. He took a drink of water.

"You good?" William was looking at him, concerned, the face of a concerned old friend, and, as George talked, William's expression didn't change, but it did seem to grow ever so slightly slack.

The script was excellent, George said, one of the best he'd seen in a long time, and there was a lot of interest, but it would be expensive and that made people jittery, William knew how it was, didn't he, and if he could say that William was attached it would make a tremendous difference to the higher-ups. "It's really less than three weeks of filming, and we could do it in L.A., if that helps."

George felt his smile wobble on his face. "You know I don't get excited about much," he went on, "and this is really one of those things. I feel it. Magic brain, right?"

William didn't say anything for a moment. He was nodding a little, staring past George. "Ah," he said finally, scratching his chin, pushing his plate away from him. "You know I'd like to work with you. You know I'd like to help out. I didn't know you were trying to get anything together."

"I wanted to catch up," George said. "In person."

"Well, good," William said. "Good for you."

Kenny appeared and removed the plates, and William straightened on his stool, energized by Kenny's presence. "Listen," he said, "send it over. I'll take a look. Okay? I'll look at it. I can't say how soon, can't make promises, but I will look at it."

"Great," George said, "that's all I ask, and you know, let me know. What you think."

Without his noticing, William had gestured for the check; Kenny placed it in front of William in its leather folder.

"I got this," George said, reaching for the bill, "it's on me," but William had somehow given Kenny his credit card already. He signed the receipt briskly, not responding to George's protests.

"Please," William said, and smiled, warmly, one hand on George's shoulder. He squeezed it once, then again. "I'm just happy to be out with my old friend."

THE THEATER WAS ONE of those single-screen places any schmuck with a camera could rent out and show his movie for a weekend. You could probably show your vacation photos. Otherwise, it screened movies that had been out for months already, finally cheap enough for the theater to afford. Benji had set up a step-and-repeat on the slushy sidewalk. A single loop of velvet rope clipped to two poles. Meager, George thought, meager. But how unkind. Rein it in, he thought—he was very drunk. He looked around for Benji but didn't see him. There were two photographers there—maybe friends of Benji's, he had no idea who else would be persuaded to come out, but who knows? They took a few photos of George and William together, William's heavy arm on George's shoulder. William was so tall. I'm shrinking and I'm old, George thought. It was a little bit funny. The camera's flash blinded him for a moment, a crack of light—all this is vapor. George stepped away so they could take photos of William by himself. He watched William in his overcoat, smiling gamely. George was responsible for William's presence there on the snowy sidewalk, in front of this step-and-repeat, being photographed by idiots. He was a good friend.

"Where's the man of the hour?" William

said, rejoining George by the door. His affect was amiable, but something had chilled, some formality had taken hold.

"I'm not sure," George said. "Maybe he's inside."

A girl in a bright orange puffer coat and bare legs came up to where they were standing; George saw William brace himself for the interruption. But the girl was smiling at George, nervously.

"Hi, Mr. Friedman."

"Hi," he said. He didn't recognize her. She had her hands in her coat pockets, craning to look past him inside the lobby.

"He's just in the bathroom," the girl said. "And I don't know, like, anyone here. Then I saw you and I was, like, thank God."

Benji's girlfriend. Maya, Mara? They'd met only once before, when Benji and she had crashed at the loft for a night, and they'd barely spoken, Benji hustling her into the guest room, leaving in the morning before George woke up. She was prettier than Benji deserved, big brown eyes, piercings up and down the ridge of her ear, an almost invisible gold hoop through her septum. Somehow the effect wasn't aggressive but pretty, delicate. She made it seem very natural and appealing for women to pierce their faces. He tried to cast back—had she and Benji met at school? Was she from Toronto? He didn't know where he'd dredged up that information.

"This is William," George said. "Benji's godfather, actually."

"Mara," she said, shaking his hand. The girl was visibly shivering, though trying to pretend she wasn't.

"Let's get inside," George said. "No sense waiting in the cold."

THERE WAS A FOLDING TABLE in a corner of the lobby filled with paper cartons of popcorn and Costco-brand bottles of room-temperature water.

"It's free?" Mara said, looking at George. "I can just take it?"

"Of course."

She brightened so instantly that he almost laughed. The popcorn was dry, a nauseating yellow, but he ate a carton anyway, standing up, plowing through handfuls without enjoyment. Mara ate hers piece by piece, plucking each one like a jewel. How old was she? Twenty?

A man with a white ponytail and tinted sunglasses gripped George's arm, pumped his hand.

"George, my man!"

He was familiar, if only foggily—had he been an editor? His shirt was unbuttoned enough that a shark-tooth necklace was visible, nestled in the fur of his chest. If George caught the name of the woman whose photo the man flashed from his phone, he had a wife named London. Jesus.

These days George found he could end conversations easily—he just went quiet, stared off into the ether. Blinked slowly. A sort of Mount Rushmore maneuver, and all the conversational energy dimmed to nothingness. The man looked at George, looked to where he was staring. The man squinted, then smiled. "Well," he said, "great seeing you."

George gave the barest nod.

—

ENTER THE SON.

"Dad," Benji said. "Dad, holy shit, I'm so glad you're here."

Benji hugged him tight, a bottle of beer clutched in one hand. His cheeks were flushed. He was wearing a Hawaiian shirt under a leather jacket, a sort of bowler hat on his head. He put an arm around Mara, pulled her in so he could kiss her on the cheek. "This is so cool, right?" He kept looking around. "And holy shit!" He hugged William. "This is blowing my mind. All of you guys here."

"This guy," he said to Mara, squeezing William's arm, "was basically like my second dad."

Mara looked at William, impressed, but George could tell she didn't recognize him.

"We were in Cabo once and we went deep-sea fishing. You remember that? How I barfed all over the deck?"

"That was me," George said. "You and I went."

"No," Benji said, "no way."

"It was me," George said.

Benji caught William's eye and they shared a look. "Sorry," he said, his voice softer, "but I remember it was this guy"—he punched William lightly in the shoulder—"because you brought circus peanuts and told me it was to catch a clownfish, right?"

William shrugged, affable. "Maybe it was your pops, huh? All that was so long ago."

But it sounded like William, it's true, the whole cutesy bit with the candy, and George knew that he was wrong, of course he was wrong, that his son's fond memory did not include him. William and Benji were talking now about some trip they'd all taken to Wyoming. Another trip he had forgotten. Or maybe this was after the divorce, a trip he hadn't even known about. They didn't notice George was silent. He ran his tongue along his teeth; the popcorn had left some residue in his mouth, some chemical dryness. He caught sight of himself in the lobby mirror; he was grimacing, his gums dull and exposed. So many opportunities, here on Earth, for embarrassment. Mara smiled at him, her blank, even smile. It cheered him a little. She was a pretty girl. What had that **Times** essay said? **I was just grateful to have been a sentient being in this world.**

THE THEATER SEATS SMELLED a little wet, everyone humping their dripping coats over the chair in front. The room was not full, not even close. Maybe seventy people. Maybe a hundred, George corrected himself, be generous. William sat on one side of him, an empty seat on the other. For Benji. Next to that, Mara sat, prim, her orange coat bunched in her lap. She had another carton of popcorn and looked almost radiant with excitement. She loved his son. His son, who was standing in the front, still wearing that hat. For an excruciating minute, Benji attempted unsuccessfully to adjust the height of the microphone stand. He kept shooting glances out at the audience, saying something no one could track.

"We can't hear you!" a voice shouted.

Finally Benji pulled the microphone off the stand entirely.

"Well, here we go," he said. "Apologies for the, uh, technical difficulties there."

He paused—it took a moment for George to understand that he was pausing for some reaction. There were a few scattered laughs, a whistle from one of his college friends.

"Ben-**gee!**" someone bellowed.

Benji dipped his head in acknowledgment.

"I just want to say, it's just a real honor to have made this film. It was a learning experience," he said, "for sure, but it was also just a really beautiful thing, a beautiful coming together of people."

Benji was visibly grooving on the sound of his own voice, on being the focus of an audience. George could remember that feeling, acutely, though you were never supposed to make it clear you liked it, and certainly not as clear as Benji was making it, peacocking back and forth, lassoing the mike cord in one hand.

"Oh, yeah, and I also wanna say thank you to all of you who helped." He paused to look out over the seats. "It was pretty much everyone in this room—either you gave us spiritual support or some of you all gave money and we just could not have done it without you."

His hands formed a kind of lumpen prayer pose around the microphone; he bowed a little in the direction of the audience.

"And a special thank you to the guy who started it all. Started my love of all this"—he gestured around the theater. George shifted, uncomfortable. Here it came.

"William Delaney," Benji said. "The one and only, here tonight and—just—wow." He beamed into the lights. "No words. A legend."

People turned to look over at them; William raised a hand, nodded genially. A phone flashed. George didn't move his face. Mount Rushmore. When people started clapping, he clapped, too.

"And last but not least," Benji said. "I want to give a shout-out to my old man. Another legend. George Friedman."

The clapping lessened slightly in volume. George sensed that people were asking one another who he was. William was smiling at him, and so was Mara. He smiled, too. These were nice people. Onstage his son mouthed "Thank you" silently. Could he even see George, sitting there, or was he only guessing, generally, where his father was? It occurred to

George that maybe he was meant to rise, to say a few words. Was there a version of this life in which he stood, delivered a speech about his son? Not this version, anyway. Whatever space might have opened up for such an occurrence closed. Benji pressed on.

"And please spread the word, get it out there. Facebook and Twitter and all that. Far and wide. We want the world to see this." He looked around, his face shiny in the lights. "Oh," he said. "And I hope you like it."

THE WHOLE THING WAS under fifty minutes. It was too long to be a short and too short to be a feature and the world would not see it—it would show nowhere except in this theater on Twelfth Street on this February night in the year 2019. Getting permission for the songs alone would have cost well into the millions—it was basically a music video of the Beatles' greatest hits. Interspersed were interviews with Benji's friends and what appeared to be many adjunct faculty members of Santa Monica City College. The sound of traffic drowned out one whole interview, someone sitting on a bench in a city park, squinting into the lens. From time to time, his son's large, ruddy face wobbled onscreen, bigger than he'd ever seen it. "The Oxford English Dictionary," Benji intoned, "defines love as a feeling or disposition of deep affection or fondness for someone." A choker shot of Benji: his weak chin, the whiff of insecurity, a rash along his jawline from shaving.

As a kid, Benji had been obsessed with all the movies that George hated, all the whammy movies, as that one producer used to call them. Act I—set up the whammy. Act II—whammy. Act III—hit 'em with whammy and more whammy. What was whammy? Explosions, car chases, shoot-outs, blood and guts. George had never touched that stuff—the tidal wave swallowing the city, the train going off the tracks. He hadn't kept up; all those effects, the CGI. A new world had crept up on him. Well, maybe he had lacked a certain tolerance, an ability to accept change. And, really, what was so wrong with the whammy stuff, the formulas? George had thought those movies were too neat, too rote. They were too easy to love. He tried to explain that to Benji, once, back when he still believed he was educating him, believed that his son would absorb these lessons and be grateful. He hadn't. And, anyway, that's exactly what Benji had loved about movies, what made him watch **Die Hard** over and over. Who wouldn't want to imagine that life might have a shape, a formula? That the years didn't just pass through you. Dark night of the soul, all is lost—then the moment of victory, the reversal, all is well, reunion, tears. The hero prevails. Dissolve to black. Roll credits.

BACK ON THE SIDEWALK in front of the theater, the streets were white. George looked up and snow streamed toward him out of the darkness. Someone had taken down the step-and-repeat. Already, the staff were setting up for a midnight showing of some other movie, a Japanese horror film. William came up beside him.

"Well," William said, pulling on his gloves. "Shall we head out?"

The after-party was at someone's loft, ten blocks away, but William begged off.

"I'm too old," he said. "Let the kids have their fun. But come on, I'll drop you."

A black car was already idling by the curb. William's driver got out to open the back door, then lingered, eyes on the ground.

The car was quiet and warm. William's arms were folded across his chest, his head leaned back. He had his eyes closed.

"Fun night," he said. "Benji's a good kid."

"Yes," George said. They wouldn't talk about the movie. George understood this was a kindness on William's part.

"You did good," William said, his eyes opening. He patted George's arm.

What sort, George could ask, of good, exactly? But instead he nodded, looked out the window. He was tired. They both were. It would be a quick drive.

AND NOW WILLIAM WAS GONE, already home, in bed next to his wife, and here was George, in this loft that belonged to a stranger. It had got too smoky at the after-party, so someone opened all the windows. Now it was freezing, George wearing his coat and scarf. He parked himself on the couch until three girls took over the other end, giggling, huddled around a cellphone as if it were a heat source. Then George idled by the doorway, hunched into his coat. He knew none of these people. Benji was pressing tequila shots on guests, his Hawaiian shirt unbuttoned halfway, sweating so much that he looked like he was melting. He was having an almost violently good time, it appeared, kissing women on the cheek, crooking his arm around his friends' necks. He was, George supposed, proud of himself. Mara was sitting on the edge of a stool, picking at a bowl of pistachios, a plastic cup of wine on the counter. She was looking at the photographs on the wall. When George took the stool next to her, she startled a little.

"Oh, hi, Mr. Friedman," she said, still chewing a pistachio.

"Having a good time?"

"Oh, yeah, totally," she said, one hand covering her mouth while she swallowed. "This is fun."

Young people didn't know how to ask questions, keep a conversation going. It would have bothered him, normally, but it didn't, that night.

"Me too," he said. Out the windows, George could see the snow falling. "I'm having a great time."

The girl looked at him, then down at her lap. Would she ever think of him, years from now, when he had ceased to exist?

"Did you like the movie?" George said.

"Yeah. It's cool to see it in an actual theater. Instead of just, like, him doing it in pieces." Mara drank from her glass. "Benjamin worked really hard on it."

"Did he?"

She nodded. "Oh, yeah, totally. All the time."

"Good," George said. "Very good."

Mara's face brightened, she was smiling, and George felt himself smile back, a reflex—but she was smiling at Benji, who'd come up behind George. He wrapped Mara in a hug, lifting her off the stool.

"Come meet people," Benji said, spinning her around, her skirt riding up as she tried to pull it down. Benji tickled her and she laughed, slapping his hand away.

"See you, Mr. Friedman," Mara said, over Benji's shoulder.

Benji turned to him, just for a moment. "You good, Pops?"

George nodded.

His son beamed. His moonfaced son, drunk and sweaty, smelling like grass. Benji. **Benjamin.** And then he was gone.

THE NANNY

"THERE ISN'T MUCH IN THE HOUSE," Mary said. "I'm sorry."

Kayla looked around, shrugged. "I'm not even that hungry."

Mary set the table, bright Fiestaware on placemats alongside fringed cloth napkins. They ate microwave pizzas.

"Gotta have something a little fresh," Mary's boyfriend, Dennis, said cheerily, heaping spinach leaves from a plastic bin onto the pizza. He seemed pleased by his ingenuity. Kayla ate the spinach, took a few bites of crust. Mary poured Kayla more water.

When Kayla asked for a beer, she saw Mary and Dennis glance at each other.

"Sure, sweetie," Mary said. "Dennis, do we have any beer? Maybe check the garage refrigerator?"

Kayla drank two over dinner, then a third out on the porch, her legs tucked up into the oversized hoodie she had taken from Mary's son's room. The wildness of the backyard made everything beyond it look fake: the city skyline below, the stars. Reception was awful this deep in the canyon. She could try to walk closer to the road again, out by the neighbor's fence, but Mary would notice and say something. She could feel Dennis and Mary watching her from inside the kitchen, tracking the glow of her screen. What would they do, take her phone away? She searched Rafe's name, searched her own. The numbers had grown. Such nightmarish math, the frenzied tripling of results, and how strange to see her name like this, stuffing page after page, appearing in the midst of even foreign languages, hovering above photos of Rafe's familiar face.

—

BEFORE TUESDAY THERE HAD hardly been any record of Kayla; an old fundraising page from Students for a Free Tibet; a blog run by a second cousin with photos from a long-ago family reunion, teenaged Kayla, mouth full of braces, holding a paper plate bent with barbecue. Her mother had called the cousin and asked her to take the photo down, but by then it had already passed into the amber of the Internet.

Were there any new ones? They had dug up photos of Kayla lagging behind Rafe and Jessica, holding Henry's tiny hand. Rafe in his button-down and jeans, surrounded by women and children. They were the only pictures Kayla had of her and Rafe together. That was strange, wasn't it? She came across a new photo—she looked only okay. A certain pair of jeans she loved was not, she saw, as flattering as she'd imagined it to be. She saved the photo to her phone so she could zoom in on it later.

Kayla made herself close the search results, then let her text messages refresh. A split-second reprieve where she could believe that perhaps the forces in the universe were aligning and aiming something from Rafe in her direction. She knew before they finished loading that there would be nothing.

"YOU NEED ANYTHING, SWEETIE?"

Mary stood in the porch doorway, just a black shadow.

"I'd turn the light on for you," Mary said, "but there's no bulb out here, actually."

Mary had been her mother's college roommate, now a drug and alcohol counselor. Kayla's mother had wanted her to fly home—I'll buy the ticket, she said, please—but then the photographers had descended on her ranch house in Colorado Springs. Waiting for Kayla. So her mother called Mary, her college roommate, Mary, the witness at her small courthouse wedding, a wedding that had been followed quickly by divorce. It was easy to imagine what Mary thought of Kayla. A waste, she probably believed, Kayla just twenty-four years old and now this. Probably, Mary thought, this was just the result of an absent father, an overworked mother.

But how could Kayla explain? This felt correct, the correct scale of things. Kayla had always expected something like this to happen to her.

"I'm fine." Kayla made her voice excessively polite.

"We're about to start watching this documentary," Mary said. "About a girl who was the first female falconer in Mongolia." She paused. When Kayla didn't respond, she kept on. "It's supposed to be very good."

Mary, with her loose linen shirts, her silver oxfords, was the kind of older woman that younger girls were always saying they wanted to be like. Mary, with her great house up in the canyons, all the seventies wood left untouched. She probably let her teenage son call her by her first name. Kayla understood that Mary was a nice person without really believing it; Mary irritated her.

"Actually," Kayla said, "I'm pretty tired. I'm just gonna go to bed."

Did Mary want to say something else? Almost certainly.

"Thanks again for letting me stay," Kayla said. "I'm gonna try to sleep."

"Our pleasure," Mary said, and hesitated, probably gathering herself to dispense some sober wisdom, some ex-junkie psalm. Before she could speak, Kayla smiled at her, a professional smile. Mary seemed taken aback, and Kayla took that moment to pick up her beer, her phone, to walk past Mary and make her way to the bedroom. Mary's son had wrapped his door in caution tape, pinned up a DANGER: KEEP OUT sign, a sticker of a nuclear symbol. Yeah, yeah, we get it, Kayla thought, you're a toxic little shit.

MARY'S SON WAS WITH his dad for the school break, and Mary had obviously tried to make the room nice: she left Kayla a stack of fresh towels, a little wrapped hotel soap, **The Best American Essays, 1993** on the nightstand. Still, it smelled like a teenager, fumes of Old Spice and cheap jerk-off lotion, unwashed sports equipment lingering in the closet. Kayla lay on the neatly made bed. The surf posters on every wall showed men, pink-nippled and tan, on boards in the middle of huge, almost translucent waves. The posters were like porn about the color blue.

Still nothing from Rafe. What to do but continue to exist? A sense of unreality thrummed under each second, a panic not altogether negative. She found herself testing out the wording, imagining how she would characterize the feeling to Rafe if he called. She felt proud of the phrase, **It's like I've been plucked out of my own life.** She said it silently to herself, and her heart pounded faster. Dramatic. As long as she was sleeping, she felt fine, as long as there was the option to blot things out—she still had a few of Rafe's sleeping pills, prescribed to him under a different name. She pulled a Ziploc from her backpack and shook out a Sonata, nibbling off a bitter shard. Best to parcel them out, save some for later. She pressed a wet finger to the bag to pick up any residue, then gave up, swallowing the second half of the pill with the last sip of beer.

There was nothing interesting to look at in Mary's son's drawers—boxers folded tightly, T-shirts from various summer camps, their specialties increasingly psychotic—rock star camp, fashion design camp. A cigar box of coins and a pair of cufflinks made from typewriter keys, a yearbook in which only girls had written. She flipped through the yearbook: the kid appeared to go to the kind of school where everyone learned to knit in lieu of taking prescription amphetamines. A well-meaning missive from a teacher took up a whole page in the back. She doubted the boy had ever even read it. She did, though, sitting on the edge of the twin bed—it was moving, strangely, though maybe it was just the Sonata kicking in, the way her thoughts took on a slurred quality, the shutter speed starting to slow.

Max: I'm so proud of you and all you have accomplished this year. Can't wait to see what you'll do in this world! You are a very special person—never forget it!

She could hear, from the living room, the sounds of the documentary, the swell of Mongolian music gaining in urgency. She would bet anything that Mary was tearing up right now, overcome by the sight of a soaring falcon or a close-up shot of an old man's hands, wind whipping across a Mongolian plain. Kayla had known a girl in college who'd been adopted from Mongolia. Her name was Dee Dee, and all Kayla remembered was that she had a tendency to shower with the curtains open, that she picked her face at the sink, leaving behind tiny shrapnels of pus on the mirror. Where was Dee Dee now?

Kayla was getting tired. She knew she should get up and turn off the light, take her contacts out, take off her bra. She didn't move.

Did Dee Dee remember her? Had she heard the news?

You are a very special person, Kayla thought to herself. A very. Special. Person.

DENNIS HAD BEEN THE ONE to pick her up. Kayla didn't even have her own car, had used one of Rafe and Jessica's. It had been one of the appealing things about the job, the car, though now it seemed very stupid, another way her life had been tethered to these people. Kayla watched Dennis approach in the Volvo—he would have had to inch through the photographers at the main entrance. He stopped at the gate and waited to be buzzed in. He was wearing a visor whose brim was gnawed with age, a fleece vest embroidered with the logo of a vitamin company. He looked like a sad and tired animal, pulling through the security gates, and Kayla felt, briefly, that she had done something terrible. To summon someone like Dennis to a place like this. For reasons like this. But it wasn't really true, was it, that she was terrible? Life is long, she told herself, opening the car door. People always said things like that, life is long.

"Is this all your stuff?" Dennis said.

"Yep."

Just one suitcase, her backpack. She had taken all of it, even the earrings Jessica had given her, the dress with the tags still on. The contents of the endless gift bags, perfume and makeup, so many lotions, a microcurrent wand, items Kayla would search out online, finding the exact retail prices, adding up the numbers until she got a little drunk. Kayla didn't feel guilty, not yet. Would she ever? The security cameras were recording her getting into Dennis's car. Would Jessica watch this footage? Would Rafe? She tried to keep a mild smile on her face, in case.

THE FIRST TIME SHE met Jessica was at the interview, after the agency had already approved her. Jessica came in late, sitting down at the table. Jessica was distracted: her necklace had caught on her sweater.

"Can you just—" Jessica gestured, and Kayla took over, gentling the latch, trying not to tug so the sweater wouldn't stretch. She was bent close to Jessica's face: her skin lightly tanned, her hair almost the same color, all her features so tiny and symmetrical that Kayla could hardly look away, absorbed in the seamlessness of Jessica's beauty. Kayla felt a curious elation—how much time she had wasted trying to be beautiful, when it was obvious, now, how impossible that was. The knowledge was almost a relief.

"There." Kayla dropped the necklace back in place, smoothing the sweater. It was cashmere, the color of root beer.

Jessica touched the chain absently, smiled at her. "You're sweet."

—

THE LATEST NEWS WAS that Rafe's text messages were connected to the kid's iPad, that's how Jessica found out, and it was amazing to imagine where this information came from, how these facts made their way to light. Because that part was true, anyway; Kayla had gotten careless about texting Rafe, toward the end, and even if he had rarely texted her back, Jessica would have seen right away what was happening.

Henry's favorite game on the iPad had been set in some virtual diner where you made hot dogs and hamburgers, a clock ticking down to zero. Kayla tried playing it once and sweated through her shirt, it made her so agitated. The burgers kept burning, the soda machine kept breaking. Customers fumed and departed.

Henry took the iPad from her with exaggerated patience.

"It's easy," he said. "Just don't pick up the coins right away. Then you have more time."

"But," she asked, "isn't the point to get a lot of money?"

"Then it goes too fast," Henry said. He seemed to feel sorry for her. "It's tricking you."

FOR HIS EIGHTH BIRTHDAY, Kayla got Henry a machine that carbonated water and a book she had loved as a child. She read it aloud while Henry stared at the ceiling. He seemed to like the book, though the ending surprised her; she had not remembered that the old man died so violently, that the orphan grew up and was not very happy. In the afternoons, when the housekeeper was gone and Henry was at school, the air seemed to go slack. It was strange to walk through the rooms, open the closets. Touching the hanging dresses, Rafe's pants, sweaters folded with tissue paper.

The thing was, she was a smart girl. She'd studied art history. Her first class, when Professor Hunnison turned out the lights and they all sat in the dark—they were eighteen, most of them, still children, still kids who had slept at home all their lives. Then the whir of the projector, and on the screen appeared hovering portals of light and color, squares of beauty. It was like a kind of magic, she had thought back then, when thoughts like that didn't feel embarrassing.

How mysterious it seemed sometimes—that she had once been interested or capable enough to finish papers. Giotto and his reimagining of de Voragine's text in his frescoes. Rodin's challenge to classical notions of fixed iconographical goals, Michelangelo's bodies as vessels for God's will. It was as if she'd once been fluent in another language, now forgotten.

Before he ate lunch, Henry got fish oil gummies in the shape of stars. Kayla liked them, too—one for him, two for her. They were covered in sugar but you were supposed to ignore that part, focus instead on the fishy fat plumping your brain and making it pinker and brighter. For lunch, Kayla made grilled cheese sandwiches on brown bread and cut apple slices. They ate outside, off paper towels. After eating, they lay in the sun in silence, Henry still in his swim trunks, Kayla in her carefully sexless one-piece.

Rafe had once pulled the crotch of that swimsuit to the side to stick a blunt finger inside her. Was that the second or the third time? Kayla imagined being the kind of person who recorded details like that in a journal. She had lots of them: Rafe liked to nap with one arm flung over his head. Rafe had scars on his back from teenage acne but told her they were from a rock-climbing accident. Strange how these were facts that would mean something to other people, too, strangers who didn't even know him. If you searched him, everything was there—his allergies, his approximate height, photos of him as a young man. She pretended never to have seen any of it. That was between them always, the pretended unknowing.

It must have been the third time, the time with the swimsuit. The sheets on the pool house bed smelled like sunscreen. Rafe had his hand on her under the sheet, his eyes closed. Kayla looked at his bland, handsome face—it was always strange to touch it, like touching the memory of someone.

"How'd you start acting?" she asked. Her voice was druggy and low, neither of them fully awake.

"I was actually pretty young," Rafe said.

There had been a visiting actor from Arts in Schools that came to perform for his class, he told her.

"You have to remember," he said, "this was Iowa, in January." It was before she had read all the articles—Rafe told the story so haltingly, she'd assumed it was some kind of secret, something precious mined up from his psychic depths.

Apparently the visiting actor had opened all the windows of the classroom, maybe to call forth some appropriate level of drama, the freezing air gusting around while he paced in front of the desks, reciting **Hamlet.**

"It blew my mind," Rafe said. "Truly."

"Cute," she'd said, imagining Rafe as a child, moved by adult things.

One night at dinner he had a piece of food in his teeth —the sight of it gave her an almost erotic discomfort until Jessica finally reached over and flicked it away. This was what she couldn't explain; Kayla hated him and loved him at the same time, and part of it was maybe he was stupid.

Later she read the story about **Hamlet**

almost word for word in many different interviews.

RAFE WAS AWAY FOR almost a month, filming eight time zones away, but as soon as Henry was on winter break, he and Jessica flew out to meet him, Kayla coming too, her pay doubled. She had her own hotel room close to the set. Outside the window, beyond the hotel's white walls, gasoline trucks made the rounds of the dirt streets.

After they arrived, Rafe barely looked at her. But, she told herself, it made sense. Jessica was always around, or some PA with a walkie-talkie appearing to "invite" Rafe to set. People only ever "invited" Rafe to do the things he was supposed to do. At a dinner for the cast, he'd pinched her nipples, hard, in the back hallway of the restaurant, his breath fumy with the local beer, flavored with kola nuts and wormwood. She laughed at the time, though waiters seemed to have noticed, along with at least one of the producers, judging by his smirk. They were actually alone only once. Jessica had sent Kayla up to their room to grab sunscreen for Henry. She opened their door, using Jessica's key card, and there was Rafe, watching a boxing match on television, the curtains drawn.

"Hi, you," she said, going to kiss him, and he fumbled, kissing her back with tight lips. Was he blushing? It was strange. Still, they had sex, quickly, her dress pushed up, the bedcovers only slightly disturbed. She went into the bathroom to wipe herself, careful to flush the toilet paper. She was still being careful then. There was the sunscreen on the counter. When she returned to the bedroom, sunscreen in hand, Rafe was absorbed by the television, his face blank, the bedcovers smoothed, as if nothing had happened at all.

IT WAS KAYLA'S DAY OFF; Jessica had taken Henry to one of the mountain towns for the afternoon. Kayla napped in the cool room, under the mosquito netting that made everything look shrouded in smoke. The first few days, she'd felt fine, but she had a delayed reaction to the required vaccines, the whites of her eyes going milky, dreams leaking into her waking life. She drank bottled water all day but still her urine was an unnatural brown color, sludgy and smelling like sulfur.

She woke from the nap groggy and hot, her sunburn pulsing. The on-set doctor had said to keep drinking water, to watch for cloudy thinking. Was this cloudy thinking, the glowy specter of Bugs Bunny in the hotel room?

You're a beautiful girl, he said.

Bugs said these things without his mouth moving. They were thoughts beamed from his brain directly to Kayla's, a shimmy in the air between them. Sometimes he did a sort of side-to-side shuffle, a slow-motion soft shoe. Everything he did was slow. Bugs Bunny. She smiled from the bed. Bugs didn't have anywhere else to be. He didn't actually say this in so many words, but she understood it, the sentiment was there in his big swimmy eyes—he would stay with her in this hotel room all day. If that's what she wanted.

I should go visit Rafe, don't you think?

She said this, or thought this.

I don't know. Bugs blinked. Is that what you want?

Bugs was so smart.

I should go. She tried to eke out another thought from her inflamed brain. I'm gonna go. I gotta see Rafe.

Bugs bowed a little—a syrupy, slow bow. If that's what you need to do.

KAYLA CHANGED INTO A dress and had a pineapple juice and vodka at the hotel bar. They were shooting by the cliffs that day, close enough that Kayla walked the ten minutes through the dunes, full of sand gnats and horseshit. Kayla sweated through her dress by the time she got to the set. Everyone was just standing around. Rafe nodded at her but didn't come over to say hi. He looked grim. They'd made his eyebrows too dark; they read clownish. Maybe they would look fine on-screen. She could tell he was irritable, hungry, antsy, wanting a shower, wanting a drink. She sensed it before Rafe sneezed, before he scratched his nose. Would he ever know this feeling? This level of precise, almost psychotic attunement to another person?

"Why are they stopped?" she asked one of the lighting guys.

He barely acknowledged her. "They found something in the gate."

"Oh. The gate?"

The guy squinted into the middle distance, shrugged. Was she imagining his curtness? No. The crew didn't like talking to her anymore. That should have been the first sign. People had an animal instinct for power, could sense that her usefulness was at its end.

Kayla settled into one of the chairs under a temporary awning outside a trailer. The sun washed out everything so it looked sketchy, unfinished. Her sunburn made her skin feel tight. She scratched her ankle, lightly. If she were just sunburned, it would be fine, but it was sores, too, these raised red bites. She rubbed her ankle against her other ankle. Gently, gently. Nothing seemed to be happening, but everyone was tense. The script supervisor was doing a crossword on his phone. She watched the makeup girl run in and press a tissue to Rafe's forehead. He submitted himself to her with great patience. He was, after all, a good actor. Kayla plucked her dress away from her armpits, but it was futile—the fabric would stain, of course it would.

THE ACTUAL FILMING WAS too far from the tent for Kayla to hear anything. She watched Rafe say something, watched him tilt his face up at the sky. They ran the scene again. What scene was this? She was waiting for them to shoot the opening sequence. The director told her, at that dinner when everyone was still being nice to her, when it was obvious she was sleeping with Rafe, to watch out for that.

"Some directors film it right away," he said, "right off the bat. But the actors don't jell yet, you see. If you wait too long everyone just hates each other, they're rushing through it. Like senior year. You time it so they're settled into their characters and still showing up."

This was only the director's second movie. The studio had given him so much money. He looked like he was twenty years old. He kept joking about how he didn't know how to do anything.

The shoot had stopped again. Rafe was walking toward her. She straightened and got to her feet.

He was sweating, his face red.

"You're sitting in my eye line," Rafe said. "I can't do the scene if I look up and keep seeing you there."

"I'm not in your eye line," she said. She could feel the makeup girl glance at them.

"You don't think you are, but it's my eye line, that's the point," Rafe said. "It's what I see. Not what you see. What I see. And I'm seeing you."

"Okay."

He widened his eyes, about to say something, then seemed to soften.

"Why don't you go swim in the pool at the hotel? Get some lunch?"

"Yes," she said. Her voice was faint. "That's a good idea."

She knew Rafe didn't want her to make a scene. And she wouldn't. She smiled out to the nothingness, the empty horizon. The land was scrubby and not beautiful, not at all how she had imagined. In truth, it was her first time out of the country.

—

KAYLA HADN'T LEFT MARY'S in three days. The one time she'd gone to the store, someone had taken photos of her filling up Mary's car with gas on the way back. Kayla was wearing aviators and looked unhappy in the pictures, her lips thin, her hair brassy and overwashed. She wasn't as pretty as Jessica. That was the obvious thing people were saying and it wasn't as if Kayla didn't also know that it was true, though she didn't know why it made people so angry at her, so personally offended. Kayla had been offered a TV interview. Compensation to drink a brand of vitamin water the next time she went out in public. An interview in **Playboy,** too, though apparently they were no longer shooting nudes.

Mary knocked lightly on the doorframe. "You good?"

Kayla sat up. "I'm fine," she said. She put her phone on the bed, screen down.

"Dennis and I are going to a friend's for dinner tonight," Mary said. "You should come."

"Oh, that's okay," Kayla said. "Really. I can hang here."

"You shouldn't be alone," Mary said. "I feel bad. Like you're trapped."

"It's fine."

Mary wrinkled her brow, her mouth in a frown.

"You'll feel better," she said. "They're sweet people. She tests recipes for cookbooks, he teaches at Occidental. It'll be a good group."

Her saying yes made Mary happy, and Dennis was beaming, too, when they piled in the car, even these minor plans animating him. He was scrubbed to a pink gleam, the short sleeves of his golf shirt hanging past his elbows. Mary drove down the narrow canyon roads, Dennis in the passenger seat, one arm around Mary. Had he been married before—did he have kids? Kayla didn't know. He seemed to exist only in Mary's orbit, the boyfriend harvesting lemons from the backyard to bring to the party. They kept glancing at Kayla in the rearview. She sat in the backseat next to the shopping bag full of lemons, a bottle of red wine. Kayla wore the dress Jessica had given her and Mary's son's sweatshirt, her hair in an unflattering ponytail. The dress was a nice fabric, a sort of linen and silk blend, the color of asphalt—she fingered the fabric, idly, where it draped across her knees. Jessica had been kind to her.

No one at the party paid her much attention. Everyone was older, busy with their own lives, with their kids who darted in and out, one wielding a plastic ukulele, another screaming a counting song in French. It was the first time Kayla had thought of it—of course there were people in the world who did not know or care about Rafe or Jessica. The food was out on a table, guests hovering with their plates. She ate some lentil salad with a plastic fork, had a watery margarita from a pitcher, a glass of white wine.

In the hallway, she passed someone dumping the last of their drink into a potted plant. She didn't know these people.

Outside was nicer. The pool was still and gave off a floodlit shimmer. No one was around. The hills were a dark mass, occasionally marked with houses. Kayla could smell the earth cooling, the clumpy chaparral that rimmed the pool, the sound from a fountain she couldn't see. She crouched down to dip her hand: the water was the same temperature as the air. Kayla sat cross-legged, her glass cradled in her lap.

She opened her text messages. The final ones from Jessica were from two weeks ago, all logistical. She looked at her saved photos, paparazzi shots of Rafe, his arms crossed. She had not seen it before, how annoyed he looked, beleaguered, surrounded by Jessica and Kayla, Henry, people who needed things from him. Poor Henry. His little shoulders, his immaculate hair. His open, wanting face.

She finished the last of her wine.

Someone opened the door. It was the daughter of the hosts. Sophie, or Sophia.

"Hey," Kayla said. Sophie crouched but didn't sit. Kayla could smell her tangy child breath.

"Are you cold?" Sophie asked.

"Nah," Kayla said. "Not yet."

They were quiet for a long moment. The silence was fine. Sophie looked younger than Henry. Her nostrils had childish rims of snot.

"What grade are you in?" Kayla asked, finally.

"Second."

"Cool."

Sophie shrugged, an adult shrug, and started to stand.

"Where you going?" Kayla touched one of Sophie's knees. The girl shifted at the contact but didn't seem bothered.

"My room."

"Can I come?"

Sophie shrugged again.

SOPHIE'S ROOM WAS CLUTTERED, a paper lantern in the shape of a star hanging over the bed. Sophie gestured at two Barbies, nude and prone under a paper towel, their fingers fused and slightly fluted.

"I made this house for them," Sophie said, indicating an empty bookshelf. One shelf had a Band-Aid box next to a Barbie lying on its side in a tight, shiny dress.

"This is the party room," Sophie said, "watch." She flipped a switch on a plastic flower keychain and it started to cycle through different colored lights. "Wait," she said, and ran to turn off the overhead light.

Sophie and Kayla stood in silence, the noise of the party beyond, Sophie's room easing from red to yellow to turquoise.

"It's pretty," Kayla said.

Sophie was businesslike. "I know."

She flicked the plastic flower off and turned the ceiling light back on. When Kayla didn't say anything, the girl busied herself with a box in the corner. She pulled out a paper mask and held it up to her face, the kind of surgical mask you were supposed to wear to prevent SARS. Kayla knew Sophie would hold it there until she said something.

"What's that?" Kayla said.

"I need it," Sophie said. "'Cause I get claustrophobic."

"That's not true," Kayla said.

"Yeah," Sophie whined through the mask. "I even have to wear it at school."

"You're teasing."

Sophie let the mask fall and smiled.

"It's a good joke, though," Kayla said.

Kayla sat on the edge of Sophie's bed. The sheets seemed fresh, a chill coming off the good cotton. Sophie was moving the Barbies from shelf to shelf, whispering to herself. It was easy for Kayla to kick off her sandals. She tucked her bare legs in the sheets and pulled them up over herself.

"Are you going to sleep?" Sophie said.

"No. I'm cold."

"You're sick, and I'm the nurse," Sophie said, brightening. "I'm actually a princess, but I was forced to be a nurse."

"Mm."

"You're my daughter. You're very sick."

"I might die." Kayla closed her eyes.

"Unless I give you the medicine." Kayla heard Sophie fumble in the room, the sound of drawers and boxes. She opened her eyes when she felt a soft object pressing against her mouth. It was a felt donut, dotted with felt sprinkles.

"I found this in the forest," Sophie said. Her voice had a low, spooky quality. "You have to eat it."

"Thank you," Kayla said. She opened her mouth and tasted the bland felt.

"I think it's working," Sophie said.

"I don't know," Kayla said. "I think I should rest for a while."

"Okay, honey," Sophie said, and patted

her cheek gently. It was nice. With her eyes closed, Kayla felt the girl lay a paper napkin over her face, the napkin getting hot with Kayla's own breath. It was comforting, to hear Sophie moving in the room, to smell the smell of her own mouth.

"KAYLA."

Before she opened her eyes, she imagined the man's voice was Professor Hunnison's. Why did this soothe her? He knew she was here. She blinked heavily and smiled. He had come to see her. He wished her well.

"Kayla!"

Kayla opened her eyes. It was Dennis, Dennis with his blousy shirt, his hairy forearms.

"You should get up," Dennis said. "Mary's been looking for you, she was worried. We're going home."

Kayla looked past Dennis but Sophie was gone. The room was empty.

"Up we go," Dennis said. He kept looking at the doorway. He wanted to leave.

Kayla felt strange. She'd been dreaming. "Where's Sophie?"

"Time to get going, okay, let's get a move on."

She blinked at him from the pillow.

"Come on, Kayla," Dennis said, pulling the covers back. Kayla's dress had ridden up and her underwear was showing.

"Jesus," he said, and tossed the blankets back over her. His face was red.

"I'm sorry," Kayla said, getting up. She pulled her dress down, searched out her sandals.

"Are you?"

The tone of his voice surprised her—when she glanced at him, he looked intently at the floor.

Kayla felt the room around her, her cheap sandal in her hand. "I'm not ashamed, if that's what you're thinking."

Dennis started laughing, but he just seemed weary. "Jesus," he said, rubbing his eyes. "You're a nice girl," he said. "I know you're a good person."

The anger she felt then, close to hatred— "Maybe I'm not."

Dennis's eyes were watery, pained. "Of

course you are. You're more than just this one thing."

Dennis scanned Kayla's face, her eyes, her mouth, and she could tell he was seeing what he wanted to see, was finding confirmation of whatever redemptive story he'd told himself about who she was. Dennis looked sad. He looked tired and sad and old. And the thing was, someday, she would be old, too. Her body would go. Her face. And what then? She knew, already, that she wouldn't handle it well. She was a vain, silly girl. She wasn't good at anything. The things she had once known—Rodin! Chartres!—all that was gone. Was there a world in which she returned to these things? She hadn't been smart enough, really. Even then. Lazy, grasping for shortcuts. Her thesis moldering in her college library, a hundred labored pages on **The Expulsion of Joachim from the Temple.** She'd messed with the margins and font sizes until she barely made the required page count. Professor Hunnison, she thought, miserably, do you ever think of me?

Dennis steered Kayla through the last gasps

of the party, toward the front door. Where had he found a brownie along the way? He held it out to her, wrapped in a napkin. Maybe he felt bad. Kayla shook her head.

Dennis started to say something, then stopped himself. He shrugged and took a bite of the brownie, chewing avidly. He checked his phone.

"Mary's bringing the car around," Dennis said. "So we can just wait here." His mouth was full, and he was ignoring the crumbs falling down his front, gumming up his teeth. When he noticed Kayla was watching him, Dennis seemed to get self-conscious. He finished the brownie in one bite, wiping his lips with the napkin. At least he had given up on the idea of lecturing her. Convincing her there was some lesson in all this. That wasn't how the world worked, and wasn't it a little tragic that Dennis didn't know that yet? Kayla smiled and sucked in her stomach, just in case—because who knew? Maybe there was a photographer, hidden out there in the darkness, someone who'd been watching her, who'd followed her here, someone who had waited, patiently, for her to appear.

ARCADIA

"THERE'S ROOM FOR EXPANSION," Otto said over breakfast, reading the thin-paged free newspaper the organic people sent out to all the farms. He tapped an article with his thick finger, and Peter noticed that Otto's nail was colored black with nail polish, or a marker. Or maybe it was only a blood blister.

"We draw a leaf or some shit on our label," Otto said, squinting at the page. "Even if it just kind of looks like this. People wouldn't know the difference."

Heddy simmered slices of lemon at the stove, poking at the pan with a chopstick. She'd changed into a sweater dress and her legs were rashy. Every morning since she found out she was pregnant, she'd been drinking hot water with lemon. "It corrects your pH levels," she'd explained to Peter. She had a glass to wash down all her prenatal vitamins, big dun-colored capsules that smelled like fish food, vitamins that promised to soak the baby in minerals and proteins. It was strange for Peter to imagine their baby's fingernails hardening inside her, its muscles uncoiling. The unbelievable lozenge of its heart.

Heddy pursed her lips sideways at her brother. "That's kind of stupid, isn't it?" she said. "I mean, why don't we just get certified, the real way?"

Otto fluttered his hand. "Got a few thousand lying around? You're certainly not contributing."

"I'm broadening my mind." She was starting her first semester at the junior college in town.

"You know what broadens after that?" Otto said. "Your ass."

"Fuck you."

"Yeah, yeah. I had to hire more people and that costs."

Peter had seen these new workers: a bearded man and a woman, who'd moved into one of the trailers a few weeks ago. They had a young boy with them.

"It all costs," Otto said.

Heddy narrowed her eyes but turned back to the pan, intent on fishing out the lemon.

"Anyway," Otto continued, "we can still say 'natural' and all the rest."

"Sounds good," Peter said, trying to be enthusiastic. Otto was already shuffling the pages, on to something new. He seemed to like Peter as much as he liked anyone. When he found out that Peter had gotten Heddy pregnant, it was his idea that Peter move in and work for him. "I guess she's eighteen," Otto had said. "No longer my worry. But if I see so much as a bruise, I'll end you."

Heddy put her hand on Peter's shoulder: "He's teasing," she said.

Peter had moved into Heddy's childhood bedroom, still cluttered with her porcelain dolls and crumbling prom corsages, and tried to ignore the fact of Otto's room just down the hall. Otto managed the hundred and fifty acres of orchard surrounding the house. The land was near enough to the coast that great schooners of fog soaked the mornings with silent snow. When it rained, the creek outran its banks, a muddy, frigid surge that swamped the rows of apple trees. Peter preferred it up here, the thousand shades of gray and green instead of Fresno with the sameness of heat and dust.

By the time he and Otto had finished breakfast—eggs from the chickens, fried in oil and too salty—Heddy had gone up to their bedroom and come down with all her things, her raincoat already zipped, a canvas backpack over her shoulder. He knew she'd already packed it with notebooks, a separate one for each class, and her chunky cubes of Post-its. No doubt she'd devised a color-coded system for her pens.

Otto kissed her goodbye, making a lazy swat at her ass as he headed out to turn the heater on in the truck, leaving Heddy and Peter alone in the kitchen.

"Heddy's off to Yale," she announced. She tightened her raincoat hood and grinned at him from the circle within. With her face isolated by the hood, she looked about twelve, the blooms of color on her cheeks tilting even more cartoonish. She slept through most everything—the dogs, the rooster, thunderstorms—and it seemed like proof of her greater moral center, something Peter could imagine existing as whole and real in her as a red apple. An innocence coupled with a strange knowingness: when they had sex, she kept looking down to watch him inside her.

"You look pretty," Peter said. "Done at four, right?"

Heddy nodded. "Home around five," she said. She loosened her hood, pulling it back to expose her hair, the tracks from her comb still visible.

PETER AND OTTO SPENT the day in Otto's truck in near silence. Otto drove the orchard roads, stopping only so Peter could dash out in the rain to open a gate, or chase down the ripple of an empty candy wrapper. No matter how much time they spent together, Peter couldn't shake a nervousness around Otto, a wary formality. People liked

Otto, thought he was fun. And he was fun, the brittle kind of fun that could easily sour. Peter hadn't ever seen Otto do anything, but he'd seen the ghosts of his anger. The first week Peter had moved in, he'd come across a hole punched in the kitchen wall. Heddy only rolled her eyes and said, "He sometimes drinks too much." She said the same thing when they saw the crumpled taillight on the truck. Peter tried to get serious and even brought up his own father, dredging up one of the tamer stories, but Heddy stopped him. "Otto pretty much raised me," she said. Peter knew their mother had moved to the East Coast with her second husband, and their father had died when Heddy was fourteen.

And they did love each other, Otto and Heddy, living in easy parallel habitation, as if the other person was a given, beyond like or dislike. They surprised Peter sometimes with their sentimentality. Some nights, they watched the movies they'd loved as children, colorized films from the fifties and sixties: orphans who could talk to animals, a family of musicians who lived in a submarine. The movies were oddly innocent—they bored Peter, but Otto and Heddy loved them without irony. Otto's face went soft during these movies, Heddy on the couch between Otto and Peter, her socked feet escaping from under the blanket. Peter heard them talking, sometimes: absorbed in long, intense conversations, their voices sounding strangely adult, conversations that trailed off whenever Peter came into the room. He'd been surprised that neither Heddy nor Otto cared that much about nudity, Otto striding naked down the hall to the shower.

When Otto talked to Peter, it was only about yield. How many tons of almonds per acre, what kind of applications they'd make to the soil in a few weeks, after harvest was over—fish emulsion. Compost tea. When they drove past any of the workers in their blue rain ponchos, up in the trees on ladders, or gathered around chubby orange water coolers, Otto would honk the horn so they jumped. One man held up his hand in silent greeting. Others shielded their eyes to watch the truck pass.

They were mostly seasonal pickers, moving from farm to farm, and a few students on leave from fancy colleges. The students accepted produce and a place to live as trade, an arrangement that Otto found endlessly amusing. "They got college degrees!" Otto crowed. "They email these fucking essays to me. Like I'm going to turn them down."

The new guy Otto had hired was different. Otto didn't even ask him if he'd work for trade. He had already asked for advances on his salary, accompanied by careful lists of his hours written on the backs of envelopes. Peter knew Otto had let the guy's wife work, too. Nobody seemed to care who watched their boy, except for Peter, who kept his mouth shut.

AROUND NOON, OTTO PULLED the truck off into a grove of stony oaks. They left the doors of the truck open, Peter with a paper bag between his knees: a sandwich Heddy had made for him the night before, a rock-hard pear. Otto produced a bag of deli meat and a slice of white bread.

"The kid from Boston asks if he can take pictures while he harvests," Otto said, folding a slice of meat into the bread. "What for? I ask him." Otto paused to chew, then swallowed loudly. "For his website, he says to me." He rolled his eyes.

"We should get a website," Peter said. "It's not a bad idea."

It had actually been Heddy's idea. She'd written about it in her notebook. Heddy's notebook wasn't expressly secret, but Peter knew he wasn't supposed to read it. It was for her self-improvement. She wrote down business ideas for the farm. Kept itemized lists of the food she ate, along with calorie counts. Wrote down what days of the week she would wear her teeth-whitening strips, what days she would jog around the orchards, ideas for baby names. She'd written the beginnings of bad, sentimental songs that confused him, songs about pockets full of rain, men with no faces. One page she'd filled with his name, over and over in ballpoint pen. It took on a new life, his name, repeated like that.

"A website," Otto said, stuffing the ham into his mouth. "Freeman Farms on the Web. Get one of the college kids to do the thing. With photos. Apples you'd want to fuck."

Otto laughed at his own joke. Under the far grove of trees, Peter could see the workers, clustered together for their lunch. Since it had stopped raining, some of them had hung their dripping ponchos in the branches, for shade.

OTTO AND PETER SPENT the rest of the afternoon in the office. Otto had Peter handle the phone calls to their accounts. "You sound nicer," he said. After Peter finished up a call with the co-op in Beaverton, Otto jabbed a chewed-up pen in his direction.

"Go find out who's gonna make our website," he said. "I want flashy shit, too, blinking lights and video and everything." He paused. "Maybe a place for a picture of us, too. So people can see who they're doing business with."

"That's a good idea."

"It makes people feel safe," Otto said. "Doesn't it? To see a face."

—

HEDDY HAD TAKEN HIS car to school, so Peter drove Otto's truck out to the trailers, the passenger seat full of the cartons of extra eggs from the chickens. The workers lived in five aluminum-sided mobile homes, the roofs tangled with wires and satellite dishes, yards cruddy with bicycles and a broken moped. He could tell which cars belonged to the college kids by the bumper stickers—they needed even their vehicles to have opinions. Otto had let the college kids pour a concrete slab by the road a few months ago; now there was a brick grill and a basketball hoop, and even a small garden, scorched and full of weeds.

As he approached, Peter saw a boy out in front of the first trailer, the boy from the new family, bouncing a mostly deflated ball off the concrete. He must have been eleven or twelve, and he stopped playing to watch Peter's truck approach. There was a shadow on the boy's shaved scalp; as Peter pulled up to the trailer, he realized it was a kind of scab or a burn, black with dried blood, thin and delicately crackled. It covered a patch of the boy's head like a jaunty cap.

A woman—the boy's mother, Peter assumed—opened the door of the trailer and stood on the concrete-block stoop, not closing the door fully behind her. She was in slippers and men's pants, cinched at the waist with a belt, and a ribbed tank top. She was younger than he would have guessed.

"Hi," Peter said, stepping out of the car. He ran his fingers through his hair. It made him uncomfortable whenever Otto sent him to talk to the workers. Peter was twenty, the same age as some of the college kids. It wasn't so bad talking to them. But the real workers, the older men—Peter didn't like giving orders to them. Men who looked like his father; their red-rimmed eyes, the hunch of the manual laborer. Peter had harvested garlic during high school summers, had driven in the morning dark with his father, the cab stinking of the magenta grease they used on their FELCOs. He remembered the way the group went quiet when they saw the foreman's truck, how it was only after the truck had fully retreated that they turned the radio up again, like even the meager pleasure of listening to music was something that had to be hidden.

"Otto said we could finish at three," the woman said, picking at her shirt hem. She was kind of pretty, Peter saw as he walked over to her: long black hair she'd braided, the blurry edge of a badly done tattoo creeping over her shoulder. She reminded him of the girls in Fresno. "It's after three," she said.

"I know," Peter said, sensing her worry. "It's fine. Otto just wanted to know if someone knew about computers. Like, how to make websites. I'm supposed to ask around."

"I know computers," the boy said, picking up the ball. The ball was marbled in a trashy pale pink, and the boy pressed it between his hands so the ball bulged.

"Zack, baby," the woman said. "He doesn't mean you."

"I know a lot," Zack said, ignoring his mother.

Peter didn't know what to say. The kid seemed sick or something, his eyes unfocused. "Otto wants a website for the farm," Peter said, glancing from Zack to the woman.

"I'm Peter, by the way," he said, holding out his hand.

The woman let the door shut behind her, walked over and shook his hand. "I'm Steph," she said. She seemed to get shy then. She put her hands on her son's thin shoulders. "Matt's my husband," she said. "The beard?"

"Otto likes him a lot."

"Matt works hard," Steph said, brushing lint off Zack's T-shirt. "He's at the store."

"Does he know anything about computers?"

"Matt's dumb," Zack said.

"We don't say that, baby," Steph said. She shot Peter a look, gauging his expression, then tried to smile. "Matt's not great with computers. One of the younger people might be better," she said, nodding her head at the trailers with the hammocks strung up in the yard.

"I'll ask them," Peter said. "Oh," he remembered, "I have eggs for you." He walked back to the car and got a carton from the passenger seat. "From the chickens," he said.

Steph frowned. It took Peter a moment to understand.

"Just extras," Peter said. "It's not payment or anything."

Steph smiled then, taking the carton. "Thanks," she said. The tattoo on her shoulder was a kind of vine, Peter saw as she came closer, thick and studded with black leaves.

Zack let the ball drop to the concrete and reached out for the eggs. Steph shook her head at him, softly. "They'll break, honey," she said. "It's best if I hold them."

Zack kicked the ball hard, and Steph flinched when it hit the metal siding of the trailer.

Peter backed away. "I'm just going next door," he said, waving at Steph. "It was good to meet you."

"Sure," Steph said, cradling the eggs to her chest. "Say goodbye, Zack."

Steph couldn't see, like Peter could, how Zack's face had tightened. Zack let one hand rise up to graze the edge of his wound. He scratched, and a quick filament of blood streamed down his forehead.

"He's bleeding," Peter said, "Jesus." Steph let out a harsh breath of air.

"Shit," she said, "shit," and she huddled Zack in her other arm, still clutching the eggs, and started pulling him toward the house.

“Inside,” she ordered, “now. Thank you,” she called over her shoulder to Peter, struggling to get Zack up the steps, “Thanks a ton,” and then the two of them disappeared inside, the door snapping shut.

HEDDY CAME HOME BREATHLESS from her day; kisses on both of Peter’s cheeks, her bags tossed on the counter. She used the office computer to look up a video on the Internet that showed her how to cover her books using paper shopping bags, then spent half an hour at her bedroom desk, dreamily filling in the name of each class, smudging the pencil with her fingertips.

“That’s the only way to get a realistic shading,” Heddy explained. “Like it?” she asked Peter, holding up a book.

“It’s great,” Peter said, naked on top of the bed covers, and Heddy’s eyes scatted down to study her drawing again. He had planned to tell her about his day, about Steph and Zack. That horrible wound. But it would make her sad, he thought, and she cried so easily now. Worried even when she had a bad dream, as if the fear would pass through her blood somehow and affect the baby.

"Le Français," Heddy said, slowly. "I got to pick a new name," she said. "For class. I'm Sylvie," she said. "Isn't that pretty?"

"It's nice," Peter said.

"I got to pick second from a list. The girls who had to pick last got, like, Babette." She erased something with great concentration, then blew the remnants away. "I have to get special shoes," she continued, "for salsa."

"Salsa?" Peter sat up to look at her. "That's a class?"

"I need a physical education credit," she said. She smiled a mysterious smile. "Dancing. Good to know, for our wedding."

He shifted. He wished suddenly that he was wearing underwear. "Who do you dance with in this class?"

Heddy looked at him. "My classmates. Is that okay?"

"I don't want some asshole bothering you."

She laughed. "God, Peter. I'm pregnant. Think I'm safe."

He decided not to tell her about Steph and Zack.

"We're going to make a website for the farm," Peter announced, lying back against the pillows.

"That's great," she said. He waited for her to say more. To say it was her idea, not his. He sat up and saw she was still bent over her books.

"A website," he repeated, louder. "One of the workers knows how to make one. He can set it up so people can order off it."

"That's wonderful," she said, finally smiling at him. "I've always thought we should have one."

"Well," he said, "I had to convince Otto. But everyone else has one. It makes sense."

"Exactly," she said. She left her books on the desk to come to the bed, to lay her head on his chest. Her weight against him felt nice, the press of her tight belly, and he kissed the top of her head, her hair that held the cold of the air outside and smelled like nothing at all.

PETER PROPPED THE FRONT DOOR open with a brick and lugged cardboard boxes of canned food and plastic bags of bananas from the car to the kitchen table. He'd been in charge of grocery runs since Heddy started school. Rainfall was the heaviest it had been in twenty years, and on the way to the house Peter stepped over an earthworm in the grass. The worm was slim, the color of bright new blood.

Peter cleaned out the refrigerator before putting the groceries away, throwing out the expired tub of baby spinach he'd bought on the last run, the leaves matted into a wet stink. He was still learning how to buy the right amount of food.

He could hear Otto moving around in the office. Otto had been working with one of the college kids on the website. They had figured out the domain name, and there were some photos up already, a form to submit orders that was almost finished. The college kid spent a lot of time out on the porch, talking on his cellphone, his fingers pinched girlishly around a cigarette.

Peter watched now as the college kid walked back to the trailers through the gray rain. In the distance, greasy smoke was rising from the brick grill. Maybe Steph was there. Peter had seen her a few times, working alongside Matt. She hadn't acknowledged him. Peter hadn't seen Zack outside the trailer again, even on sunny days.

Peter bought a notebook for himself on the grocery run. He'd meant to write in it, like Heddy did. Record his ideas, his thoughts about the world. He splayed it across his knees and waited with a pencil, a glass of water. But there was nothing he wanted to say. He wrote down what Otto had told him about living well on an acre, what plants to buy. What trees could grow from cuttings. What sort of drainage you'd need. He would need to know these things when he and Heddy got their own place. He let himself imagine it: no trailers crudding up the property. No Otto leaving commas of pubic hair on the toilet seat. Just him and Heddy and the baby. He put the notebook aside. The water in his glass had gone stale. He picked an apple from the bowl on the table and flicked open his pocket knife, making idle cuts in the apple's skin. It would be hours before Heddy came home.

Soon he started carving designs, words. It pleased him to get better at it, to let whole sections drop cleanly under his knife. He carved his own name over and over in loops he linked around the core. Liking the reveal of wet flesh against the red skin. He lined up the finished apples in the refrigerator, where the rotting spinach had been.

He napped on the couch and dreamt about Heddy dropping a glass, the two of them watching it explode blue and low on the ground. He jerked awake. It was dark already. Otto came into the kitchen and flicked on the light. He opened the refrigerator and burst out laughing.

"You are losing your mind."

Peter looked up from the couch. Otto swung two apples by their stems, Peter's cuts withered and browning, wrinkled at what had been their sharp edges.

"Do you work only with apples? Or is there room to branch out? I'm talking oranges here, pears," Otto said. "I'm just proud you're keeping busy."

—

PETER GOT UP WHEN he heard the car outside. His shirt was wrinkled but he tucked it in as best he could.

"It's freezing," Heddy said, hurrying through the door without a coat on. Her hair was dripping onto her shoulders, her raincoat bunched in her arms.

"Look," she said. She held out the raincoat. "Mold," she said, flinging it to the floor. "Crazy, huh?"

She didn't wait for Peter to answer.

"I'll have to get a new one," she said, kissing him quickly. She tasted like chlorine. She'd started swimming after class in the school exercise center. Low-impact exercise, she called it. She said it was good for the baby. Peter tried not to think about her body exposed to strangers in her swimsuit with the high-cut legs. How the seat of her swimsuit sometimes wedged itself into her ass. She got home later and later these days.

"How was swimming?"

"Fine," Heddy said. Her hair was dripping all over the floor and she didn't seem to notice.

"You've always sucked at swimming," Otto

said to Heddy. He tore one of the plastic bags of bananas open with his teeth. He tried to peel a banana, but only mushed the top. Heddy reached over and grabbed the banana from Otto.

"It's easier to open it from the bottom," she said, pinching the stubby end so the peel split cleanly under her fingers.

Otto narrowed his eyes at her, snatching the banana back. "Thanks, genius," he said. "Glad to know you're learning so much. **Voulez-vous coucher avec moi** and all that shit." He turned to Peter. "Sam fixed the home page," he said. "All the pictures load now."

"Good," Peter said. "I told the co-op they could start ordering online in a week or so. They seemed happy."

Heddy ignored both of them, kicking her raincoat in the direction of the trash can. Each time she parked on campus, it cost ten dollars, and Peter knew she kept meaning to buy the parking pass that would save her a hundred bucks. Last week she told him, finally, that she'd waited so long that the pass was no longer a good deal. She seemed to feel this had been a great failure on her part, the failure to buy the parking pass in time.

Heddy set water to boil for her tea, then arranged herself at the table to do her homework. She'd gotten a bad grade on her first French test, and had seemed perplexed and hurt ever since. Peter didn't know how to help her.

Otto was telling Peter some story about one of the workers, some RV they wanted to park on the property.

"And I tell him, sure, be my guest, if you can even drive that thing," Otto said. "I guarantee you it won't start up again so easy."

"Can you guys go outside?" Heddy said, finally looking up at them. "Sorry," she said. "I just—I have to call someone for school. On the phone."

IT WAS COLD ON the porch, the air thick with the smell of wet earth. Peter hunched into his coat. Otto was still talking, but Peter wasn't listening. He looked up at the sky but couldn't orient himself. When he tried to focus, the stars oscillated into a single gaseous shimmer and he felt dizzy. Even from the porch he could hear Heddy inside on the phone. She was speaking halting French to someone she called Babette. He felt ashamed for suspecting anything else. She kept breaking into English to correct herself.

"I know," Heddy said. "She is **très mal.**" Her accent was clumsy—he wished he hadn't noticed. Through the windows, Peter saw her pacing the kitchen, her familiar shape made foreign by the pocked glass.

Otto paused his monologue to study Peter.

"Where's your head at, brother?" Otto said. "You look like you're off in space."

Peter shrugged. "I'm right here."

Inside, Heddy said a final **"Bonne nuit."** Peter watched as she gathered her books and headed up the stairs, her shoulders a little hunched. Her ass was getting bigger, a humble sag that moved him. She turned out the lights as she left, like she forgot anyone was even out there.

PETER HAD THOUGHT IT was coyotes, the whooping that woke him up. He stood at the window of their bedroom, feeling the cool air beyond the glass. The ragged calls filtered through the dark trees and had that coyote quality of revelry—his father used to say that coyotes sounded like teenagers having a party, and it was true. He hadn't spoken to his father since he'd left. But Peter had Heddy now. Maybe, soon, a house of their own that they'd live in with their baby, the curtains for the nursery that she'd want to sew herself.

The idea pleased him, and he glanced over. Heddy was still sleeping peacefully, her mouth open. She'd taken a bath before bed and a dark stain spread across the pillow from her wet hair. There was something new in her face, though, some cast of resignation, since the bad grade in French. At least she was still going to classes. She made a face when he'd asked about registration for next semester, as if even that was uncertain, though classes would end a month before her due date.

A dog had disappeared a while ago; Heddy swore it had been coyotes, so Peter knew he would have to go downstairs to make sure the three dogs were tied up, that they hadn't left any of their food uneaten. He pulled his boots from under the bed and found his hat. Heddy turned over but didn't wake up.

The dogs were fine, up on their hind legs when they heard Peter coming. They whined and pulled their chains, dragging them heavily on the ground.

"You hear the coyotes?" he asked them. Their food bowls were empty and silver, smelling of their breath. "You scared?"

The noise came again, and Peter stiffened. The coyotes were so human-sounding. He whooped back, crazily.

"Ha," he said, scratching the dogs. "I'm scary too."

But the noises doubled then, and Peter could make out, in the mass of the cries, what sounded like whole words. He could see, far off in the orchard, car headlights turn on abruptly on one of the dirt roads, casting a smoldering wash of light on the surrounding land.

"Fuck." Peter looked around. Otto's truck was gone; he was probably in town. Peter hurried to his own truck and started the ignition, then jumped out to untie one of the dogs, an Australian shepherd that Heddy had named, to Otto's disgust, Snowy.

"Up," he said, and Snowy leapt into the cab.

Heddy had taken the truck to school, and it smelled like wet clothes and cigarettes, the radio turned up full blast to the staticky dregs of the country station. She hadn't told him she'd started smoking again. Peter knew she wasn't supposed to smoke—pregnant women couldn't smoke. But suddenly he wasn't sure. Because Heddy wouldn't smoke if it could hurt the baby, he told himself. So maybe he had it wrong. Peter fumbled with the volume knob, turning the radio off, and took the ranch roads as fast as he could without headlights.

The strange headlights he had seen were still on, but the car wasn't moving. As Peter got closer, he slowed the truck, but he knew whoever it was had heard him. His heart beat fast in his chest, and he kept one hand on the dog.

Peter was close enough that his own truck

was lit now. He parked and felt around under the seat until his hand closed around a short piece of broken rebar. "Hello?" Peter called from the truck. The headlights of the other vehicle hummed steadily, and specks of bugs swooped in and out of the twin columns of light.

Peter climbed out of the truck, the dog following.

"Hello?" he repeated.

It took him a moment to understand that the other truck was familiar. And before he had understood it fully, Otto walked out from the darkness into the bright room made by the headlights.

He was drunker than Peter had ever seen him. He wasn't wearing a shirt. He looked to the air around Peter's face, smiling.

"Peter," Otto said. "You're here."

Behind him, Peter saw two women giggling in the orchard. He could see that one was naked, a plastic camera on a strap around her wrist. He noticed the other woman's T-shirt and see-through lavender underwear before realizing, in a sickening moment, that it was Steph, her dark hair sticking to her face.

"Steph and I made a friend," Otto slurred. "Come on," he said to Steph and the woman, impatient. "Hurry up."

The women held on to each other and stepped gingerly through the grass toward the trucks, the woman with the camera shorter than Steph. They were both wearing sneakers and socks.

"I know you," said Steph, pointing at him. She was drunk, but it must have been something else besides alcohol. She couldn't quite focus on Peter, and she smiled in a strange, fanatic way.

"Hi," said the plump girl. Her hair was blond and worn long with jagged edges. "I'm Kelly. I've never been to a farm before."

Steph hugged Kelly, her small tipped breasts pressing into Kelly's larger ones. She said loudly into Kelly's ear, "That's Peter."

Otto kept licking his lips and trying to catch Peter's eyes, but Peter couldn't look at him. Snowy ran up to the women and they both shrieked. Steph kicked at the dog with her dirty tennis shoes as he tried to nose her crotch.

"Don't kill 'em," Otto said to Snowy. "I like 'em."

"Come on, dog," Peter said, patting his leg.

"You aren't going, are you?" Otto leaned against his truck. "Help me finish this," he said, the bottle in his hand sloshing.

"Don't go, Peter," Steph said.

"I told them they'd only drink the best," Otto said. He held out a bottle of grocery-store champagne to Peter. "Open it for the girls."

The bottle was warm. Snowy was agitated now, circling Peter's feet, and when Peter twisted the cork and it shot into the dark, Snowy yelped and took off after it. Steph grabbed the bottle from Peter, the bubbles cascading down her arms. Kelly clicked the shutter.

"See?" Otto said. "That was easy."

"Steph," Peter said. "Why don't I drive you back to your house, okay?"

Steph took a long drink from the bottle. She regarded Peter. Then she let her mouth drop open, bubbles and liquid falling down her front. She laughed.

"You're a disgusting girl," Otto said. Snowy

came to sniff at his boots, and Otto gave him a heavy kick. The dog whimpered. "A disgusting girl," Otto repeated.

"Hey, shut up," Kelly said, meekly.

"Fuck you," Otto said, smiling hard. "Fuck. You."

Peter started to move toward his own truck, but Otto came over and pushed him back, one hand steady on his chest.

"Come here," Otto said to Steph, his hand still on Peter. "Come on."

Steph turned her back on Otto, pouting. Her buttocks through the mesh underwear were shapeless and crisscrossed with impressions of the ground.

"Oh, fuck off," Otto said. "Come here."

Steph laughed, then took shaky steps toward Otto. He caught her and shoved his mouth against hers. When they pulled apart, he clapped at her ass. "Okay, now kiss him."

Peter shook his head. "No."

Otto was smiling and holding Steph by the hips. "Kiss him, babe. Go on."

Steph leaned over so her chapped lips brushed Peter's cheek, her body pressed against his arm. The shutter clicked before Peter could back away.

"Listen," Peter said. "Why don't you guys go somewhere else?"

"Really?" Otto laughed. "Go somewhere else. Interesting suggestion."

Peter hesitated. "Just for tonight."

"I own this fucking property. You are on my property right now."

"Otto, go home. Let's go to sleep. This isn't good."

"Good? Don't you work for me? Don't you live in my house? You fuck my sister. I have to hear that shit." He pushed Steph away. "You think you know her? Do you even realize how long Heddy and I lived out here alone? Years," he spat, "for fucking years."

HEDDY WAS STILL ASLEEP when Peter came into the bedroom, the room navy in the dark. He took off his clothes and got in bed beside her. His own heartbeat kept him awake. The house was too quiet, the mirror on Heddy's childhood vanity reflecting a silver knife of moonlight. Could a place work on you like an illness? That time when it rained and all the roads flooded—they'd been stuck on the farm for two days. You couldn't raise a baby in a place like this. A place where you could be trapped. His throat was tight. After a while, Heddy's eyes opened, like his hurtling thoughts had been somehow audible. She blinked at him like a cat.

"Stop staring at me," she said.

He tried to put his arm around her, but she'd closed her eyes again, nestling away from him, her feet soothing each other under the sheets.

"We need to get our own place."

His voice sounded harsher than he'd meant it to, and her eyes startled open. She sat up, and he saw the shadowed outline of her bare breasts before she groped for the blankets and pulled them tight around her. It struck Peter, sadly, that she was covering her breasts from him.

He took a breath. "I could get another job. You could be closer to school."

She said nothing, staring down at the

covers, worrying the fake satin border with her fingers.

He suddenly felt like crying. "Don't you like school?" he said, his voice starting to unravel.

There was a silence before she spoke. "I can just work here. For Otto." She started to turn from him. "And where am I ever going to speak French anyway?" she said. "You think we'll take the baby to Paris?"

THE NEXT MORNING, PETER woke to an empty room. Heddy's pillow was smoothed into blankness, the sun outside coming weak through the fog. From the window, he could see the dog circling under the shaggy trees, the row of trailers beyond. He forced himself to get up, moving like someone in a dream, barely aware of directing his limbs into his clothes. Downstairs, he found Otto on the couch, his shoes still on, fumy with alcohol sweat. A pastel quilt was pushed into a corner, and the couch pillows were on the ground. Otto started to sit up when Peter walked past. In the kitchen, Heddy had the tap running, filling the kettle.

"And on the couch, you'll notice my dear brother," Heddy said, raising her eyebrows at Peter. There was nothing in her voice to indicate she remembered their talk the night before, just a faint tiredness in her face. She shut off the faucet. "He smells like shit."

"Morning, Peter," Otto said, coming into the kitchen. Peter worked to keep his gaze steady and level on the tabletop as Otto pulled up a chair.

Heddy padded toward the stairs with her mug of lemon water, glancing back at them. Otto watched her go, then went to the sink and filled a glass with water. He drank it down, then drank another.

"I'm in hell," Otto said.

Peter didn't say anything. A band of pressure built around his temple, a headache coming on.

Otto drank more water in huge gulps, then opened the cupboard. "Do you forgive me?"

"Sure."

Otto closed the cupboard without taking anything out. He turned to Peter, then shook his head, smiling. "Shit. 'Sure,' he says. Listen," Otto continued. "I'm meeting these guys today who've been emailing. They want to work. You have to meet them, too."

The headache was going to be a bad one, a ghosted shimmer of the overhead light starting to edge into Peter's vision. "I don't think I can," he said.

"Oh, I think you can," Otto said.

Peter didn't speak. Otto went on. "So we'll meet here. Or do you want me to tell them we'll meet in town?"

Peter pulled at his collar, then let his hand drop. "I guess town," he said.

"Easy," Otto said. "Wasn't that easy?"

They finished their breakfast in silence. The room got stale with quiet, the air pressing in, air that seemed a hundred years old. Heddy stooped to kiss Peter goodbye, her bag over her shoulder. He noticed she had put on slashes of dark eyeliner that made the whites of her eyes brighter. Peter forced himself to smile, to kiss her back.

"Lovebirds," Otto called, his hands held up to frame Heddy and Peter.

Heddy stood to leave, pulling away from

Peter. The faint smell of cigarettes lingered in the air where she had just been. Her hair was pinned up off her neck. She had on a light jacket instead of her old raincoat, and when she turned back, at the door, to wave, her gaze seemed to slide right off Peter. She looked like a new person, like no one he knew.

NORTHEAST REGIONAL

CLOSE TO FIVE HOURS ON THE TRAIN. And then twenty minutes by taxi from the station to the school. He would have time to call the lawyer, work through the options. He had the number of a consultant, in case Rowan needed to apply somewhere else. Maybe the school legally had to contact the college he'd got into, but Richard wasn't sure. And maybe it wouldn't come to that. The school wouldn't want to make anything public. The thought calmed him—good, good. They were on his side, even if they had not said so in so many words: they weren't stupid.

The trains were housed underground, in cool alleys of concrete, and Richard headed for the first car. It was only half full, the interior air recirculated to an unnatural chill. Richard settled in, that brief moment when he could present himself anew in the context of this narrowed world. He could be kind, he could be neat and conscientious, and all it took was laying his folded jacket on the seat beside him, tucking his newspaper into the webbed nylon pocket.

Richard's pills were in his bag, consolidated in one container. He could easily identify them by shape and color, the pills for depression and insomnia. Offering nudges in his mood like the touch of a dance partner, a subtle but real pressure. He felt for the pill tube through the bag's front pocket—there it was—and he was reassured, lightened.

The car filled slowly. Newcomers maintaining a zone of polite privacy, choosing seats and shaking out their newspapers as if they were making a bed. Everyone excessively tidy, excessively generous. Passing their gum silently into a napkin held to their mouths. No matter that, an hour into the ride, all solicitousness would be forgotten, music leaking through headphones, bawling phone conversations, children racing down the aisle.

A sullen girl and her father were stopped in the aisle beside him, waiting for a man to hoist his luggage. The girl stared at Richard, a fresh zit between her brows like a third eye. She was maybe fourteen, a few years younger than Rowan, but how much more childish she seemed than his son. Her gaze was unsettling, too specific—Richard looked down at his phone.

There was bad service underground, no reassuring stair-step bars on his screen, but once the train started moving he could make calls. He reread the email from Pam. Then the lawyer's email referring the consultant. "She's very good," he'd written. "A real pro." Nothing from Ana. Poor Ana, her weekend ruined. She had tried her best to be a good sport. That was the phrase he was sure was circling down at the bottom of her thoughts, stern ticker tape: be a good sport be a good sport be a good sport.

—

HE AND ANA WOULD have had a better time if they could've gone in the water. If it had been summer, they could've gone in the water, and that would've helped, but it wasn't summer, so they didn't. They sat with their backs against the base of a driftwood fence that marked someone's beachfront rectangle. The sand was baked and pale, the sea dark. Ana held his hand loosely, her face shaded under a floppy white hat. Richard had the thought that she might have bought the hat specifically to wear this weekend, and the idea made him wince.

They had lunch in town, an endless lunch. Richard could not catch the waiter's eye, and the plates lingered too long, the silverware dirtied and askew, and who wanted to stare at the soiled instruments of their feeding? The white wine tasted like granite. Ana stepped outside to call her husband. Richard could see her from the table, pacing in the courtyard. She touched her collar, turning away so her face was hidden.

She returned to the table, tore a roll in half, and soaked it in oil. She chewed energetically, her enthusiasm without veil. She piloted the conversation: work, work, a problem with a tenant who wouldn't vacate a house. Bad health news from a cousin on the West Coast. Richard's responses were clipped, but Ana didn't seem to notice, taking time with her lunch: she ate normally, sensibly, free from darker hungers. "How's Rowan?" she asked. Richard had not got the call, not yet, so he felt no anxiety at the mention of the name—Rowan was doing fine, he said, his grades were fine. Though he saw Rowan's grades only if his ex-wife sent them to him, never mind that he paid the tuition.

The waiter came by to see if they wanted dessert.

"Should we?" Ana asked, breathlessly, the waiter grinning in practiced collusion. Richard couldn't bear to enact his role, play at naughtiness.

"If you want," he said, lightly, forcing himself to erase any impatience from his voice. But Ana picked up on it anyway.

"Nothing for me," she said, handing the menu back to the waiter, making a face of cartoonish regret. You don't have to apologize to him, he wanted to say. The waiter really doesn't care. Then he felt bad for being unkind. He squeezed her hand across the table; she brightened.

HER HUSBAND WAS OUT of town for the entire weekend, and this was the first time they had spent the night together. Everything seemed significant to her—the groceries she put in the fridge, the movies she had downloaded to her laptop, that hat. Stress had caused a haze of pink to cloud her eyes, a mild case of conjunctivitis that she tried hard to downplay. Every four hours, she tipped back her head and squeezed a dropper of antibiotic into each eye.

Richard didn't need to do it, but he did—sought out these married women, the ones who looked at him across a table of catered tournedos and cut peonies while their husbands talked to the people on their right. Women whose lingerie was haunted by the prick of the plastic tag they'd tried to snap off so that he wouldn't realize it was new.

They were the type of women whose own sorrow moved them immeasurably. Who wanted to recount the details of their worst tragedies in the lull after sex. Ana hadn't seemed like that kind of woman. She tended to all her own weaknesses, briskly removing her own underwear but never taking off her watch. Like the other married women, she always knew what time it was.

She was a real estate agent, one of her listings the house in which they were staying. It had been Richard's mother's house, until she died, and was now his. He had never liked visiting his mother here, on the occasions he did, and there was no thought of keeping the place.

The afternoon they'd first met, Ana had been optimistic about the property. "It's nice acreage," she said. "Big but not too overwhelming." She walked ahead of Richard, opening doors, passing through rooms, turning on lights and faucets. Wearing tailored shorts, so that her nice legs showed.

The second time: Richard's hands loose on Ana's head as she gamely kneeled. They were outside, on the back porch, Richard's ass pressing into the slick plastic slats of a lawn chair as he tried feverishly to imagine someone watching. He said thanks, when it was over, as Ana discreetly spat into the grass.

"Really," Richard said. "That was great." Ana's smile was crooked. It was summer then, and behind them the massed green of the trees moved in silence. That was the thing about being with married women, how hidden pockets of the day were suddenly revealed. The slightest pressure and the grid buckled, exposing the glut of hours. It was only eleven and he still had the whole day ahead of him.

Back in the city, she came over at strange times, carrying a gym bag that stayed untouched by the door. Her husband, Jonathan, was an importer of olive oil and other things kept in dark, cool warehouses. Ana said his name often when she was with Richard, but he didn't mind. He was glad for the helpless invocation of her real life—he didn't need a reminder of the limits, the end already visible from the moment she had first shaken his hand, but maybe she needed a reminder. The groceries she'd brought this weekend worried him, the purity of their domestic striving, and so did the questions about his son, the assumption that Richard was tracking the saga of her cousin's health. How she had made up the bare mattress with the sheets they'd brought, eager as a new bride.

They would go back to the city the day after next, and Jonathan would return from wherever Jonathan had gone and the house would sell and all shall be well, all manner of things shall be well—the phrase surfaced in his brain, some hippie scrap that Pam used to incant to herself.

IT WAS DARK OUTSIDE, the sky faltering to black. Ana squeezed a dropper of her antibiotic into one eye and then the other, then shut her eyes tight. "A minute," she said, eyes still closed. "Tell me when a minute is up."

Richard was putting the dishes away.

"A minute," he said, after a while, though he'd forgotten to check, and she opened her eyes.

"They feel any better?" he said.

"Yeah," she said. "Lots." She was a smart

woman. She had sensed some shift in his attention and was now willfully cheerful, cool, not giving away too much. Her bare feet kneaded the cushions. She'd plugged in her laptop, and a menu screen was queued up for a black-and-white movie that he didn't want to watch. "Someone could take down this wall," she said, nodding at the room, "and then have their dining table in here."

"Someone could," he agreed.

"That's Rowan?" she said. There was a framed photo: Rowan, a few hours old, in Pam's arms.

"Yeah."

Ana got up to look more closely. "She's pretty."

He wanted to tell Ana that there was no need to catalog Pam's attractiveness, or try to gauge Richard's feelings for her—nothing residual remained. They'd been divorced sixteen years. She lived in Santa Barbara, had married again and divorced again, existed only as a voice on the telephone arranging logistics or relaying information.

"Is he sad you're selling the house?" Ana said.

It took him a moment. "Is Rowan sad?"

“He must have had fun here. In summers and stuff.”

Richard wiped his hands on his pants; there were no dishtowels.

“We only came here a few times. Rowan likes the city better, I think. I don’t think he cares.”

Pam and Richard had divorced when Rowan was two. Pam had moved to the West Coast—really, since then Richard saw Rowan only in summers, and then for only the few weeks the boy wasn’t at camp. But they had been good times. Good enough—Rowan a small stranger who’d arrive for the summer, dark-eyed and bearing a Ziploc of vitamins from Pam with detailed instructions for their distribution. With his private ways and ritualized habits, one summer obsessed with a leather wallet some boyfriend of his mother’s must have given him.

RICHARD FELL ASLEEP DURING the movie, snorting awake with his head on his chest. Ana laughed, a little unkindly. “You snore,” she said. “I didn’t know you snore.”

"It's still going?" he said. The actors on the screen had soft-looking faces; he had no idea what was happening.

"We aren't even halfway through," she said. "You want me to go back?"

He shook his head, forcing himself to stay awake. The movie finished to violent trumpets, THE END scrolling in gilded, overblown script. She shut her laptop in the middle of a horn blast.

"Bed?" he said.

She shrugged. "I might stay up."

She wanted to talk, he could tell, itching for him to push back, probe for the source of her discontent.

"I have to sleep," he said.

Ana rolled her eyes. "Fine," she said, stretching out her pretty legs without looking at him, her youth the ultimate trump card.

ALONE IN THE UPSTAIRS BEDROOM, Richard took off his pants and raked his fingers through the hair above his belly. He left his boxers on, swimmy white cotton that Ana hated, and pulled just the top sheet over himself. Where had Ana even found that movie, and what logic had made her think he would like a black-and-white movie? He was only fifty. Or fifty-one. He fell asleep.

"Hey."

Ana was shaking him, pushing his shoulder. "Richard."

He recognized her voice, dimly, a ripple on the water, but didn't open his eyes.

"Your phone," she said, louder. "Come on."

IT HAD VIBRATED, she told him, an incoming call, and she had ignored it, except it happened two more times. Richard sat up and took the phone, dumbly: Pam. Three missed calls. He oriented the time: it was only ten in Santa Barbara. But one A.M. here—Rowan. Something to do with Rowan. He was still half asleep, a bad feeling only beginning to make itself known.

"Is everything okay?" Ana said, and he started; he had forgotten her, the stranger on the bed, staring at him with her pinkish eyes.

He went down to the kitchen to call Pam back. "Richard, Jesus," she said, picking up on the first ring. "He's fine, fine, totally safe," and Richard told himself that he had never thought otherwise, though immediately his mind had zoomed through a pornographic strip of every evil thing that could have befallen his son. "The school called—I don't really understand, they aren't telling me anything. He's fine, but they need one of us there. Some trouble, a fight or something."

There was a pause. "I was sleeping," he said. "I'm sorry."

Pam sighed. "I can't get there until Monday," she said. "Why do they have these schools out in the middle of nowhere?"

"But he's fine."

"He's fine. I guess someone got hurt. He was involved, or so they said."

As a child, Rowan had not liked violence. He found the tightest corner of every room and folded himself there.

"Have you talked to him?"

"He didn't say very much. It's hard to tell."

Richard pushed a finger between his brows.

"Those people at that goddamn school," Pam said, off on a tear. As she talked, he spotted Ana in the doorway, listening while trying to appear as if she weren't, her eyes cast carefully down.

"I'll go up," he said, interrupting Pam. "First thing."

Ana snapped to attention—here was information that affected her, and she tried and failed to hide her disappointment.

THE TRAIN MOVED AT a forgotten pace, quaint. He had taken the train often when he worked for the Treasury Department, ten years before. The express, with regulars heading straight to their usual seats. The train rattled along with all the carnival heave and huff. Passing houses, boxy and plain, with aprons of lawn, the hedges sheared neatly like military haircuts. Rowan's school used to require such haircuts. Uniforms, too. Dark gray, worsted wool, jackets with rows of brass. But that was fifty years ago. Now it was scrubbed of any implication of violence, less like a school and more like a coed holding pen, funneling students into Ivy League and liberal arts colleges—there was no focus on anything beyond college itself, the first fact of acceptance.

The invitation to a party when the party was incidental. Rowan had got into a better-than-expected college—Pam was surprised and pleased—its website a well-designed labyrinth of photographs and italicized quotes in a vaguely corporate color scheme.

The boy wanted to study international relations, but that seemed to mean he wanted to study abroad and drink in new countries. He didn't exhibit any interest in Richard's work, apart from a desultory question or two, offered out of nowhere.

"How much money do you make?" he'd asked Richard once.

Richard didn't know whether to lie, whether other parents had some complicated moral arithmetic about these things. He told Rowan the truth, embellishing slightly—the year would pick up, he was sure—and Rowan seemed appropriately impressed, his eyes going cold and adult as he processed the information.

Richard had not thought of Rowan so much in a long time, not this condensed concern. He called him every once in a while, or pinged off a series of texts, Rowan's responses shorter and shorter until the exchange trailed into virtual silence—**How are your classes? Fine.** They were useless missives, but he felt he had to make these offerings. If there was a reckoning, a moment when they demanded to see the record, he could present these messages. Proof that he had tried. Ana would be driving back to the city now. He'd sent off a quick text to her as the train pulled out, apologies that the weekend had ended so abruptly, but there was still no word from her. Maybe she hadn't seen it. Or maybe she was sulking. She was a childish woman, he thought, and let himself feel free of her, glad for the escape Pam's call had offered. He drank water from a plastic bottle. He checked his phone again. He would meet with the headmaster in the afternoon.

Richard was going to wait until the train was halfway there to take a pill. This was the kind of rule he was only foggily aware of, the patter under the surface of his waking brain. But the rules were easily bent by obscure rationalizations. A cold look from a stranger, a rumble of hunger or impatience, discomfort: any of these could tip Richard into a sudden certainty that he deserved to have the pill now. So he uncapped the tube and didn't acknowledge what he was doing until he was already staring into the abundance. Oval, he decided, after a moment. He washed the pill off his tongue with a slug of water, swallowing hard. When it dropped, there was no more doggy-paddling against the riptide of the day—he could relax, let it pass over him. Clicking in like rails.

HE WAITED TEN MINUTES for a taxi: none appeared. All around him, people streamed off to the parking garage or hustled to the cars of loved ones, cars that arrived like magic and painlessly collected their cargo. Passengers sorted themselves into their proper places, trunks slamming. Richard checked his phone—still nothing from Ana, Christ. It was almost noon, clouds beginning to condense overhead.

Richard went to ask the attendant at the parking garage about taxis. "One'll show up," the man said, and Richard stalked back to the curb, his bag thudding into his side.

Finally a burgundy minivan pulled up. Richard exhaled loudly, though no one was there to hear him. The driver had long hair and rimless glasses, and hustled to open the trunk.

"I'll just keep my bag with me," Richard said.

"Sure," the man said, bobbing from foot to foot. "Sure. You want to sit up in front?"

"No," Richard said, after a moment of confusion. Did people ever want to sit in front? Though, now that he was getting in the back, he understood that some people did sit in the front, or the man wouldn't have asked. What kind of people? People who wanted to advertise their own goodness. He didn't care if the driver thought he was a shitty person because he didn't want to ride alongside him.

When he gave the name of the school, the driver turned to the backseat.

"Do you have the address?"

Irritation prickled up Richard's scalp. "It's the only school around," he said. "You don't know it?"

"Sure I do," the driver said, churlish now. "I just wanna plug it into the machine, see, it'll tell me the best way to go."

This was why you lived in cities—abundance buffered you from the vagaries of human contact. If this had happened at home, Richard would have got out and grabbed the next cab. But here he was forced to sit as the man fumbled with his GPS, forced to encounter the full, dull reality of this person. He sat back and closed his eyes.

"All set," the driver announced. Richard picked up a punitive lilt in the man's tone, but when he opened his eyes the car was moving and the man was silent, staring ahead.

THE SCHOOL WAS AT the top of a hill, overlooking the town, the swift-moving river spanned by a stone bridge. The campus buildings were gray limestone, tidy and stark. It had snowed a few days earlier, it seemed, but not enough to be picturesque, and in the muddy aftermath everything looked cheerless.

Rowan was supposed to meet him in front of the chapel, but he wasn't there. Richard should have stopped first to stow his bag at the one inn in town, with its basket of Saran-wrapped corn muffins at the front desk. He had been to the school twice before: dropping Rowan off the September of his freshman year, and picking him up for a single, awkward Thanksgiving.

He moved his bag to the other shoulder, checked his phone. An hour until his meeting with the headmaster. Rowan wasn't answering texts or calls. Richard glanced at his phone's blank screen—the galactic space of it, the empty hum. How often was he checking? Ana hadn't texted even once. He typed another note to her. **All okay here.** He watched the cursor blink—he erased the message.

He stood there for another few minutes before a boy and a girl ambled toward him, the boy not immediately recognizable as his son. It was Rowan, obvious now as the boy got closer, and Richard pretended he'd known all along. Wasn't that what parents were supposed to do? Be able to spot their children in a crowd, in an instant, the most primal of recognitions?

"Father," Rowan said, half smiling. His

son had never called him Father, even when he was a little boy. He wore a shiny jacket that seemed borrowed from someone else; his wrists strained in the too-small sleeves. Richard looked from the girl to his son. He went to hug Rowan, but stuttered, a moment of hesitation, and his bag dropped down his arm and he had to reshoulder it, an awkward lurch, and in that time the girl thrust out her hand.

"Hi, Mr. Hagood," she said.

Before Richard could understand who she was, she was shaking his hand. She had washed green eyes, thickish animal hair that fell to her waist.

"Hi."

"Livia," Rowan said. "My girlfriend."

Richard had never heard anything about a girlfriend. He stared at Rowan. "Why don't you and I talk alone for a minute?"

"We can talk in front of Livia. Right, babe?"

A dormant headache pulsed back to life. "I think we need to talk," Richard said. "Alone."

"Come on," Rowan said. "She's great."

Richard could feel Livia watching them.

"I'm sure she's great," Richard said, trying to keep his voice even. "And I'm sure she can excuse us for a moment. Right, Livia?" He forced a smile, and, after a moment, the girl shrugged at Rowan and ambled a few feet away. She breathed into her cupped hands, studiously looking away when Richard glanced over.

"I'm meeting with your headmaster in less than an hour," he said.

Rowan's face didn't change. "Yeah."

"Is there anything you want to say?"

Rowan was staring past Richard, his arms folded and straining against the jacket sleeves. "It wasn't a big deal," he said, and smiled. Out of discomfort, Richard told himself, and he felt it, too; a grimace tightened his own face. Rowan seemed to take this as some kind of collusion, and his posture relaxed. He pulled out a pack of cigarettes and lit one with a teenager's elaborate casualness.

"Don't smoke," Richard said. "It can't be allowed?"

Rowan let the cigarette hover a moment in the air, the smell rising between them.

"Frisch doesn't care. And there's worse things than smoking," he said, taking a drag. "It's not even that bad for you."

Richard's hands flexed, then relaxed. What could he do, snatch the cigarette away? His headache was worse. The pill was wearing off, the granularity of each minute becoming more apparent. He wanted to check his phone. His son kept smoking, his exhale threading thinly through the air before breaking apart. The girl was stamping her feet now, her puffy boots making her legs above them seem tiny and breakable, and Richard imagined, for a second, snapping them clean. He cleared his throat. "Where's the headmaster's office?"

PAUL FRISCH HAD ATTENDED the school as a teenager, back when it was still single-sex. His time there had been slurred over by distance until it seemed blessed, four years steadily knit with hearty friendships and kindly teachers and good-natured pranks. No matter that he had been somewhat unpopular, occasionally the recipient of pointed abuse, once punched so hard that he vomited in a tidy unreal circle in the snow. They pushed his face into his own warm sick. It was easy to forget, though. And enough had happened on the other side of the fulcrum—a scholarship to college, a sensible girl who became his wife, her long hair worn in a single braid. He'd returned to teach at the school for many years before taking over as headmaster. This office with its oak furniture and mullioned windows. A life tipping toward good, and it was only this kind of thing, the occasional meeting of this sort, that called up a sour whiff from the back of his throat, a familiar feeling elbowing its way to the light.

The student: chubby with the helpless bulk that came from psychiatric drugs, not from excess of enjoyment. Thatchy hair, like the nests that deer make in grass. He wasn't unattractive, just raw, all there on the surface. Frisch had met with his parents that morning. The boy's mother looked older than she was. A high flush on her neck, a darty, wild look. Her husband kept one arm around her in a weary huddle.

They were decent people, unable to imagine or prepare for anything like this.

And now here was Rowan Hagood's father, wearing a wool overcoat that smelled like the cold air, a man who kept tilting his phone in his lap to check the screen, as if Frisch couldn't plainly see what he was doing. Frisch shifted in his chair, the leather seat giving off a flatulent squeak that triggered an old self-consciousness. Rowan's father was hearty, at first, ready to find a solution, to cooperate. He had a full head of hair and the aggressively pleasant affect of someone used to getting what he wanted. Smiling a contained, respectful smile, a smile that assumed a shared interest here.

Rowan could not stay at the school, though his father seemed to expect otherwise. Not even the most rabid of parents with the most rabid of lawyers could have kept Rowan there. Frisch repeated the facts. As he went on, the man's heartiness started to fray, and he began passing his phone from palm to palm with increasing agitation. Frisch laid out the time line they had pieced together, what the hospital's report had concluded.

Rowan's life was not ruined. In lieu of expulsion, he and the others would be asked to leave. Rowan would be given the chance to transfer somewhere else to finish the semester. Colleges wouldn't be notified, the incident never part of any formal, accessible record. This was the best possible outcome for Rowan, Frisch explained, and Mr. Hagood should be grateful that his son's future was intact. All this would recede in Rowan's life, Frisch knew, a blip easily calcified. People like Rowan and his father were always protected from themselves.

Earlier that morning, before the other boy's mother and father had left his office, the mother had stopped and looked at Frisch. "He'll be all right, won't he?" she asked, her voice unraveling.

Frisch had assured the parents that their son would be fine. They needed to hear him say it. Everything would be okay. And how could he say otherwise—confess that he had spoken with the boy a few hours after everything, had looked into the boy's black, roving eyes, and that he couldn't say what would happen later, what any of this would mean?

—

RICHARD DESCENDED THE DARK, narrow stairs that led to the dining room of the one fancy restaurant in town. White tablecloths and stiff lace curtains—this was a part of the country where somber stood in for formal. Rowan and Livia followed behind at the respectful but vaguely menacing distance typical of bodyguards and teenagers. Their whispers were punctuated only by the girl's grating laugh. The kids had been twenty minutes late meeting him at his hotel, but the restaurant was mostly empty, Richard's reservation an unnecessary urban habit.

Pam had cried on the phone when he called her after the meeting, though Richard was careful to repeat what the headmaster had said: Rowan would still go to college; this could all be dealt with soon enough. There were logistics to get through, but it was fixable. Richard didn't fill in the blanks in the story. Didn't flesh out the incident in full, obscene detail—details the headmaster seemed to linger over, studying Richard's face as he recounted the whole thing. Like he wanted Richard to feel bad, like Richard should be the one to offer an apology. And he did feel bad—the story was awful, perverse, made his gut tighten. But what could he do now, what could anyone do? He apologized, pitching the wording carefully—enough to acknowledge that the incident was bad but not enough to encourage any kind of future lawsuit.

The waitress handed out menus while Rowan and Livia scooted their chairs closer together. Rowan had obviously told her that he would have to leave the school—when the kids had finally shown up at Richard's hotel the girl's eyes were swollen from crying. Livia seemed fine now, no lingering sadness that Richard could discern. If anything, she was fizzy with secret hilarity, she and Rowan exchanging significant glances. They started to giggle, bizarrely, keeping up some coded conversation that he didn't try to follow. Crescents of sweat were darkening the underarms of the girl's shirt. Richard tipped his phone onto the table, casually, so he could tell himself he wasn't really checking. Still nothing from Ana. His stomach hollowed and he picked at his napkin. He made an effort to smile at Livia, who looked back blankly with a shake of her uncombed hair.

Rowan had taken the news stoically, with a maddening tilt of his head as he stared past Richard out the window of his dorm room. He twisted a lacrosse stick in his hands while Richard talked, an in-and-out roll that kept a white ball trapped in the net. The movement was unusual, hypnotic, a kind of witchy glide. In the corner, his roommate's humidifier motored away, loosing puffs of dampness.

Rowan's nonchalance doubled Richard's headache. "You understand this could have been much worse," Richard said.

Rowan shrugged, keeping the ball in the net. "I guess."

This was his son, Richard kept reminding himself, and that fact had to be bigger than anything else.

"We will always help you," Richard said, conscious of trying to gather some formality, a sense of fatherly occasion. "Your mother and I. I want you to know that."

Rowan made a noise in the back of his throat, the barest of responses, but Richard saw the mask drop for a second, saw a quick flash of pure hatred in the boy's face.

—

RICHARD KNEW HE SHOULDN'T drink with the pills, but he ordered a beer anyway.

"Actually," he said, "gin and tonic."

Ana had told him once that clear alcohol was the healthiest—she drank vodka. Ana, with her nice legs and practical shoes and her skin, soapy and pale as a statue's.

"I'll have one, too," Rowan said, sending Livia into a fit of giggling. The waitress looked at Richard for permission.

"No," he said. "Christ."

The rage in Richard grew and fizzled, easy as taking a breath, easy as not responding. He stuffed his mouth with a slice of bread, dry and lacking salt, and chewed intently.

AFTER THEY ORDERED—the girl got the most expensive thing on the menu, Richard noted—he stepped out to the parking lot. "I'll be back in a minute," he announced to the kids. They ignored him. The river was close enough that he could hear it.

He called Ana. Pushing the button quieted some immediate anxiety, dropped it down a notch. He was taking action, he still had some control. But the phone kept ringing into space. Now the anxiety had doubled. It rang too many times. He felt the silence between each ring. He hung up. Maybe she had just been surprised by his call—they didn't speak on the phone, as a rule. Or maybe she had her phone on silent, or maybe Jonathan was home early. Maybe. Or maybe she was just ignoring him. Back at her apartment, doing nothing, wearing her unflattering sweatpants, her dingy bra. Revulsion caught in his throat.

Richard knew he shouldn't call again, but it was so easy to endure the same series of rings. He pressed the phone to his ear, wondering how long the rings could possibly go on. There was a moment, a click, when he thought she had answered—his stomach dropped—but it was only her voicemail. The recording made her voice sound eerie and far away. In the silence that followed the beep, he tried to think of something to say. He could see his breath.

"Cunt," he said, suddenly, before hanging up.

—

HE RETURNED TO THE TABLE, bending to retrieve his napkin from where it had fallen on the floor. An oblique thrill was animating his movements, a buoyant flush. The food arrived quickly, the waitress smiling as she set down the plates. Richard ordered a second drink. When the waitress left, Rowan stabbed a finger at her retreating back.

"Lizard person," he announced. "Two points." Livia started laughing again.

Richard just blinked, the drink a wave he was riding, another on its way. This was his son sitting beside him at the table? All is well, he thought, and all shall be well, and all manner of things shall be well.

He sawed at his pork loin, salting the mashed potatoes, loading up his fork. Rowan had ordered the pasta—claiming to be a vegetarian, which seemed like another joke of some kind—and he ate steadily, his lips coated with oil. Livia sipped at her water and poked at her steak. She cut up some of the meat but only moved the pieces from one side of the plate to the other. Rowan was in the middle of a sentence when Livia quickly shifted one of the slices onto his plate. He looked down, but kept talking.

"Listen," Richard said to Livia. He hadn't meant to speak at all. "You can't just drink water for dinner."

Livia stared at him.

"You have to eat something," Richard said.

"God," Rowan said. "You aren't eating that much, either."

"I'm just fine," Richard said. His son looked tense. Richard could tell that his hand was on Livia's knee under the table. "I'm fine," he repeated, "but I won't allow Livia to starve."

"What the fuck?" Rowan said.

Richard had never hit his son, not once. His mouth filled with saliva, and there was a pounding behind his eyes. Across the table, Livia still stared at him.

"Eat your food," Richard said. "We aren't going anywhere until you eat."

Her eyes got wet. She picked up her fork, clutching it hard. She stabbed at a thick slice of steak and brought it to her mouth, chewing with tight lips, her neck surging when she swallowed. She took another bite, her eyes widening.

"God, stop it," Rowan said. "It's fine."

Livia kept eating. "Stop, babe," Rowan said, grabbing her wrist, her mouth still cartoonishly full. She dropped her fork, letting it clatter onto the floor.

"You're a prick," Rowan said, glaring at his father. "You were always such a fucking prick."

The waitress hurried over with another fork, her face frozen in a frenzy of politeness that meant she'd seen the whole thing.

"Sorry," the girl said, tears dripping into her lap.

"No problem," the waitress sang, "no problem at all," replacing the girl's fork, bending to snatch the soiled one off the floor. Smiling hard but not making eye contact with anyone. When she retreated, leaving Richard alone with his son and the crying girl, it occurred to him, with the delayed logic of a dream, that the waitress must have thought he was the bad guy in all this.

MARION

CARS THE COLOR OF MELONS AND tangerines sizzled in cul-de-sac driveways. Dogs lay belly-up and heaving in the shade. It was cooler in the hills, where Marion's family lived. Everyone who stayed at their ranch was some relative, Marion said, blood or otherwise, and she called everyone brother or sister.

The main house jutted up from the ranchland, as serene and solitary as a ship, crusted with delicate Victorian detailing that gathered dirt in its cornices and spirals. The first owner had been a date heiress, Marion told me, adored and indulged, and her girlish fancies were evident in the oval windows that opened inward, the drained pond that had once been thick with water lilies and exotic fish. Palm fronds fell crisped from the trees that flanked the house's exterior. All the landscaping was now like an afterimage, long grown over but visible in the heights of grass, in the lines of trees that extended a path to the front door, bordered by white plaster columns.

We spent most of our time in the airy rooms of the main house. We watched the babies there, cradled them and sang, dangled glass beads on strings over their damp faces. We put together whatever puzzles were around, baroque castles or glossy kittens in baskets, starting over as soon as we had finished. I found a book on massage, with foldout graphs of pressure points, and we practiced: Marion lying on her stomach, her shirt pushed up, me straddling her and moving my hands across her back in firm circles, my palms slick and yellowed with oil. Marion had just turned thirteen. I was eleven.

My mother was going through a phase then, having night sweats and blackouts. She paid people to touch her: her naturopath, who placed warm fingers on her neck, her breast; the Chinese acupuncturist, who scraped her naked body with a plane of polished wood. I ended up at Marion's for weeks at a time, my clothes mixed in with hers, her half brother stealing small bills from me, her father, Bobby, kissing Marion and me good night square on the mouth.

One afternoon, we sat on the front steps of the main house, sharing a root beer and watching her father dig pits in the yard. Later, he would line them with leaves and fill them with apples.

"I need cigarettes," Marion moaned, passing me the bottle. I sipped the root beer with adult weariness. "Let's ask Jack for some," she said, not looking at me. Jack was Bobby's friend, visiting from Portland. He was rangy, the pale hairs on his arms neon against his tanned skin. He had been staying in the barn with his girlfriend Grady, who wore long skirts and ribbons around her ponytail. At dinner, when Grady lifted her arms to retie her bow, I saw dark hair under her arms and averted my eyes.

"It's not like it's a big deal. He'll share," Marion said, pinching a thread from the hem of her cutoffs. Marion was wearing her shorts over her favorite bright orange bikini, nubby fabric stretched tight across her breasts, her shoulders shining from sunscreen. I was wearing a swimsuit top, too, borrowed from Marion, and all day I had felt an anxious thrill from the strange feeling of air on my chest and my stomach. Marion raised her eyebrows at me when I didn't answer. "We're wearing these 'cause it's hot, okay? Don't worry so much."

Men stared at her when she wore that suit, and she liked it. When Jack first came for dinner at the ranch, he would follow Marion with his eyes when she got up from the table. That day, when Jack watched Marion in the barn as he rolled a cigarette for her, I felt a flint of heat in my insides. When he glanced at me, I turned and hunched my shoulders, trying to relieve the strain of my breasts against the borrowed fabric. I never went out in that swimsuit again.

NONE OF US KNEW then that bark beetles were tunneling in the trees, laying millions of eggs that would wipe out millions of trees. Bobby was warning of an attack so great that the United States would fold in on itself like a fist. It was the men's job to protect the women. Everyone who lived at the ranch was storing things, freezing food in huge, unbelievable quantities and clearing brush out of old Indian caves and catching water there in jugs. Bobby wanted to build a stone tower, forty feet high and circular, on top of a hill where the energy was paramagnetic and auspicious. They circled the site with silk flags and burning oils before they started construction. Marion and I watched from the hillside, slapping the mosquitoes on our legs. He was storing arms, Bobby said, for the wars, and we never quite knew if he was joking or not. Marion rolled her eyes at him all the time, but swallowed the foul-tasting Coptis tincture he gave us each morning for regular bowel movements and thick hair. "Like a pony's," he said, and twisted Marion's braid around his wrist.

Her family staked their marijuana plants on south-facing hillsides and planted them with sage and basil. They told their friends they had thirty plants, but they had five times that many, hidden all over the ranch. They sold to a dispensary in Los Angeles, and sometimes, if my mother was away for the weekend on an extreme juice fast, Marion and I were allowed to drive down with Bobby when he dropped it off. Marion's mother, Dinah, taught us to use a vacuum sealer on the plastic around the dope.

"Put on gloves," Dinah said, tossing me an old gardening pair. "If you guys get pulled over, they'll sniff your fingernails for resin."

We triple-bagged the weed and packed it into backpacks. Dinah put the backpacks into big duffel bags and covered them with beach towels, swimsuits, folding chairs, and a crate of overripe pears to hide whatever smell was left. Marion and I piled into the backseat, holding hands, our bare thighs sticking and skidding on the leather seats. We drove along the winding coastal roads, through shantytowns and orchards that drooped in the heat, past dry hills and that distant purple ridge, the cows standing motionless in the middle of a field.

—

I HAD BEEN DOWN south before, but my mother and I had driven on I-5, not the back roads. My mother would never have stopped at the rock shop, where Bobby let us each buy a piece of agate, or the date farm, where an old man made the three of us milkshakes. They were thick and I sucked at the straw until my mouth ached. Marion finished hers first, then rattled the straw around in her empty cup. She rolled down the window, got my attention, and let the cup tip and fall out of the car. When I looked back, the cup was bouncing silently into the weeds.

"Hey," Bobby said, turning half around in his seat. He swatted at Marion, but she swung her legs out of reach. "Don't do that," he said. I was smiling, like Marion, but when Bobby's voice rose, I stopped. "Don't toss shit out of the car when it's full of pot," he bellowed, slapping his hand toward Marion. His hand glanced off her bare thigh and I saw it redden. "You wanna get us pulled over for something stupid?" he said, turning back to the road.

"God," Marion cried, rubbing her leg. "That hurt."

Bobby wiped his hands on the steering wheel. He glanced back at me in the rearview and I looked away.

"They just love to get you for stupid shit like that."

I smiled when Marion looked at me. She wrinkled up her face, jokey again, but I saw her grip her agate.

I held my own agate up to the light of the car window. It was smooth, a pale blue, banded with delicate threads of white. The woman at the rock shop said it was for grace, for flight. "Good for protection," she said, when I brought it to the counter. "Blue lace agate can help you call on angels. Also heal eczema, you know, if you get dry skin."

The agate Marion picked out wasn't smooth. It was jagged and bright. Flame agate, the woman called it. "See?" she said, lifting it, turning it in her fingers. "Looks like a coal, huh? Like a hot coal."

"What's it gonna do for me?" Marion asked, reaching out to touch it.

"Well, it's good for night vision," the woman said. "Addiction, too, but you're young for that. You know what?" she said, looking at Marion. "It's just a good earth stone. For power."

"They're all like that," Marion said. "All-protective, all-powerful, blah." She grinned at the woman. "Are there any bad stones?" she said. "Like, that give you weakness or stupidness or something?"

"Yeah, or cancer," I ventured, rewarded by Marion's quick snort.

The woman glanced at me as if she was disappointed, and I looked away. The woman handed Marion and me little silk pouches. "Don't leave them in direct sunlight," she'd said as we left. "Drains their power."

WHEN WE STOPPED TO get gas, I watched Bobby at the pump, pulling uncomfortably at his waistband. I realized that it was one of the first times I'd seen him fully dressed: He wore athletic pants made of a shiny material, borrowed sneakers, his arms crossed stiffly over the sports logo on his T-shirt.

In the backseat Marion was tossing her agate from palm to palm. "Sorry Dad yelled," she said. "It's just tense. The drive."

"It's fine," I said. "Really. I don't care."

"He can be a jerk." Marion shrugged, and concentrated hard on catching the agate.

"Yeah."

Marion stopped. "He's really great, too," she said, narrowing her eyes. "He's a really great father," she said. We both looked up: Bobby snapped the wipers out of the way and started dragging a squeegee wetly on the windshield. Through the water and soap, the road beyond was blurry and far-off.

"I don't think he's a jerk." I lowered my voice. Bobby was bunching up paper towels. "I would never think that."

We heard the high squeak of glass. Bobby had scraped the last of the water away, and the world outside the car was clear again: the clapboard of the small convenience store, the propane tanks, the highway, near and empty and without end.

BOBBY DROPPED THE WEED off at a Japanese temple in Burbank. While the men did business, Marion and I flicked murky water at each other and watched the goldfish in the driveway fountain gape and flash in the sun.

"There are no rules," Jack said, back at the ranch. He showed us anything we wanted in the barn, let us pick up mouse bones, old spinning tops. Potted garlands of bulbed plants, sweet succulents we pierced with our fingernails.

"Don't feel like you have to ask to touch anything," he said. He let us look through pulpy books with black-and-white photographs of dead bodies, of bloody sheets.

"Oof," he said, twirling his fingers. "I knew Beau before he hooked up with them. He wrote poems. Sweet, bad poems."

From Jack we learned about runes, about the Ku Klux Klan. About Roman Polanski. That men who wore rings on their thumbs were liars. When Jack excused himself to the outhouse, Marion rummaged through Grady's underwear in the bureau.

"Don't look through her stuff," I said. I liked Grady.

"He said we could touch anything," Marion said. "Whoa," she crowed, holding up a pair of black lace underwear. She stuck her fingers through a slit in the crotch and wriggled them. "Crotchless panties," she laughed, and flung them at me.

"Gross," I said. When I tossed the underwear back to Marion, she shoved them deep into her back pocket. She looked at me, daring me to say something, then moved on to the **Playboys**, turning each page, discussing the women.

"This one's real skinny, but her tits are big. Like me. Men love that."

Another page, a tawny woman with an Indian cast to her face. Then the cartoons, somehow more lurid than the photographs: the bursting shirts and rounded rears, the unzipped fly.

—

A THIRTEEN-YEAR-OLD GIRL. WE talked about that a lot, what the girl might have looked like, how Roman Polanski knew her, how it had happened. Did she have breasts? Did she have her period yet? We were jealous, imagining a boyfriend who wanted you so bad he broke the law. We were drifting through whole weeks, making bonfires at night, eating twenty Popsicles in a row. We made a game of hiding the wrappers—rolling them into balls and wedging them in the crotches of trees, folding them into the pages of Jack's old almanacs and religious encyclopedias. We sat in the back of Bobby's pickup as he drove the gridded vineyards and released wrappers from our clenched fists like birds.

MARION WAS MY FIRST best friend. I never had the framed photos that girls like to give each other. I had never worn friendship bracelets, or even hated anyone else with another girl. My life seemed like something new and unasked for, Marion smiling at me in the sunshine, letting me wear her woven ankle bracelet for days at a time, braiding my hair that had grown colorless and thick, full of dust and the peculiar smell of heat. Bobby often walked around wearing a sarong low on his hips, and sometimes naked, and so none of the other girls in the seventh-grade class were allowed to visit, but Marion liked it like that. She pierced my ears one night with a needle, holding a piece of cold, white apple behind my lobe, and there was hardly any blood at all. She helped me trace the outline of my face in lipstick on the bathroom mirror, so we could determine my face shape (heart) and the most flattering haircut (bangs, which she cut with Dinah's nail scissors). Her hot breath, blowing the small cut hairs out of my eyes.

WE SPENT MORE AND more time at the barn. Marion said that it didn't make sense to wait until a trip to town for cigarettes, or mentholated pastilles, when Jack would give us both for free. Marion would stare at him while he typed at his desk, on a computer he ran with extension cords to the main house, and we passed whole afternoons looking through his shelves, murmuring among ourselves, sitting Indian-style on the floor. Marion smiled at him with an intensity that made her look almost cruel. I tried to smile that same way.

Marion leaned up against his desk and told him about the boy who had a seizure and shat himself at the community pool. "The mommies got all the kids out of the water real quick after that," she said, and waited for Jack to laugh.

Marion had told me to watch him and tell her later if I thought he liked her. So I hung back, fingering the rows of books and geodes, spooning cold tomato soup into my mouth from a mug. I took note when Jack looked at the door or at Marion's slim thighs in cutoffs.

Marion started volunteering to deliver messages from Grady in the kitchen to Jack in the barn, or ice-cream sandwiches in the peak hours of heat. I wondered if he could feel us watching him.

I never told Marion about the time I saw Grady and Jack naked, stretched out side by side on a picnic table in the yard. "We're charging ourselves," Grady laughed, her eyes closed. "By moonlight." Dark hair spread across her thighs and up her stomach like a sleeping animal. Jack smiled lazily, his hand on her.

MARION BORROWED DINAH'S OLD Kodamatic and took me up into the hills, where she stripped and had me take pictures of her naked body laid out on rocks. "You'll be good at this, I know it," she said. She tied a red ribbon around her throat like she had seen on one of the girls in **Playboy.** She closed her eyes, opened her mouth, and put her fingers on her flushed chest. I thought she looked really great, but she also looked dead. When we pulled the film out of the camera, letting it dry in the sun, some faint blue shadows spread on her chest and throat.

Marion tucked the photos into a box with a twenty-dollar bill, and she cut off a piece of her hair to put in there too, tied with the red ribbon. She said that was what Jack would want, that she could tell he was courtly and would understand the significance of it. She said her father had told her how hair and teeth had tightly wound cellular structures that held power. A tooth would be better, she said, and she opened her jaw wide and let me look inside her pink mouth. She pointed at a tooth on the top row, said it was loose anyway, from when she'd tripped, and that she'd been working on it, tonguing it to make it even looser, pressing it as hard as she could stand with her fingers. It would be out soon, she said, and she would give it to Jack and he would know for sure.

WE DAUBED VITAMIN E oil in swaths under our eyes, so that a pale glossy light caught and shone there. We looked like bright-eyed lemurs in the bathroom mirror.

"We're staying away for a few days," Marion said, looking at herself, running a finger around her lips, across the swell of them. I knew she was thinking how beautiful her mouth was, because I was thinking it, too. "You keep men on their toes. You make them miss you."

We planned our return to the barn: what bras we would wear, what we would say. Marion had written Jack's name on her body, on the bottoms of her feet, where the ink slid into the whorls. I saw it all when we changed for bed.

THE WOMEN WERE DRYING branches of lemon verbena and sage on tin sheets all over the yard, and a puppy Jack had dragged home from town kept nosing the sheets over. Marion was reading **Archie's Double Digest** with her back against a rock wall, and I was pressing tiny sequins onto my nails with glue. The day was hot and I kept dropping the silver disks into the dirt. Marion picked a scab on her upper arm, put it in her mouth, chewed it for a while, then spat it out.

"That's disgusting."

"You're disgusting," she said, turning the page. "Fuck, they don't do anything but buy hot dogs and keep girls away from Archie."

The heat of the day lay on the grass like a blanket. I tried to get the puppy's attention, but some kids were tugging at it.

"Who do you think is prettier?" Marion asked, looking thoughtfully at her comic.

"Betty. I don't know. She's nicer."

"She dresses like your mother. Which do you think Jack would like?"

"Both," I said. I had a sequin poised over my nail but was watching Marion to see if she'd laugh. She stood up suddenly.

"Let's take photos today," she said. "I need to get them in the box."

WE PEDALED THE OLD BICYCLES, bouncing roughly over gravel and ruts in the path. I carried the camera on my shoulder. Marion stood up on her pedals, her legs tan, flexing. We coasted to the lake, the water thrumming with dots of flies, scrims of algae ringing the banks.

"Let's make these good," Marion said, briskly.

"You should do whatever and I'll take the picture."

"No," she said, breaking up a clot of weeds with a stick and looking back at the main house. "You should be in them today."

I took off my clothes and folded them neatly on the bank. Marion put my hands on top of my head, and pulled strands of hair down in my eyes. She wedged a finger delicately between my teeth to show me how far to keep them parted.

"You look good," Marion said, her face hidden by the camera. She was taking pictures from far away, squatting in the dirt.

"You look young, really great."

Then she came close with the camera, so close she touched the lens to the tip of my nipple, then cracked up and collapsed on the grass.

"It's hard," she gasped.

I started to step into my cutoffs, but Marion leapt up and came toward me. She threw her arms around my neck, loose like a child, and kissed me with her eyes open. "It's okay," she said. "Pretend I'm Jack. Look sleepy. Look sexy. Try to look like I do." We were breathing hard. "Get my tooth out," she said.

She pointed to the jagged-edged thing in her mouth that moved when she touched it.

"Do it with your hands," she urged.

Marion was smiling. Both of us were, like

idiots. I tried but couldn't get a grip. Marion drew my fingers farther into her mouth. I was delirious. She picked up a rock and put it in my hands.

"Do it," she slurred, then took my fingers out of her mouth. Her hand was shaking. "Just hit it once, hard."

I looked at her; the witchy colors of twilight on her face, her eyes gone filmy and blank. Her mouth gaped, the tooth already outlined with blood.

"Just do it," she breathed.

I lifted the rock and gave a tap. "Wait," she said, recoiling. She took a deep breath. She opened her mouth then, so I could hook my fingers on her jaw. I tapped the tooth again. "Nnnh," she said, but I hit harder and felt it give. The blood covered her chin. She just stood there, stunned, cupping her mouth with her hands.

By the time I was dressed, Marion was pedaling away.

WHEN I GOT BACK to the house, she wasn't there. The puppy shuffled its nose against my foot. Bobby walked past with sheets of gray felt in his arms.

I knew enough not to look for her. I went instead to the main house, to the kitchen, where it was cool and dim and they had the radio playing. Dinah was cooking and Grady was milking a whitish liquid from plant stalks, pulsing her fingers along the stems. They were both flushed and generous, touching me affectionately as they passed. Grady motioned for me to come sit by her.

"You and Marion should be rubbing this on your faces twice a day," she told me. "You'll never get wrinkles, ever."

I smiled at them both, beaming when Grady applied the plant liquid in gentle, thorough circles under my eyes, around my mouth, between my brows. Dinah picked through beans, shuffled the wizened ones to the side, finding the hidden rot, while I sat at the counter and cut up some tomatoes from the garden. They had sunscald, their skin tight, and underneath was the hum of warm weight. I broke them open and the seeds dripped out over my hands.

Marion never showed up for dinner. I

drifted off by myself, napping in the trundle bed I shared with her, in my underpants under the coolness of her sheets. I woke disoriented in the evening light. Dinah was downstairs, calling my name.

WHEN I WENT INTO the kitchen to find her, Dinah cornered me. She grabbed me by the arm and pulled me toward her.

"Marion said you kissed her. She said you hit her." She was crying and shaking. I thought of the woman sorting the beans, the sun in her hair, and how different she looked now.

"Marion showed me her mouth. You stupid little girl."

Grady came in behind Dinah, and turned on the kitchen lights—the sudden illumination was worse, somehow, than the dark. Grady looked upset. I tried moving my shoulders but Dinah held them tight.

"You think this is normal?"

She shook a picture of Marion at me, the one of her with a ribbon around her throat and her legs spread open. I covered my mouth with my hands, but Dinah had seen me smile. She shoved her face hard against mine, so her mouth was in my hair. "I know," she said, into my ear. "Don't think I don't know who this was for."

GRADY HEFTED MY DENIM backpack into the bed of the pickup and bent down next to me in the passenger seat. "Don't worry," she said, but her voice was strained. "Just give it a few days. It'll be fine."

Dinah came out of the house, one of Bobby's old sweaters wrapped around her. She and Grady talked to Bobby while I sat with my head back against the seat, looking out at the yellow grasses. The fields were hazy with buckwheat and it was almost fall again. How had we missed the buckwheat? How had we not seen the smear of it in the hills?

"Just tell her mama we need a break for a while," Dinah said. "Just say we're going through some family stuff."

"Her mother's never around."

"Just say, I don't know, something. I don't care," Dinah said.

I saw Dinah stalk off in the side mirror, and Bobby got into the truck and started it without saying anything. I watched the lights of the main house recede behind us, the barn rising darkly against the sky, then disappearing.

My face was wet and I was hiccupping, but I didn't feel like I was crying. I couldn't tell why my forehead was wet, too, my ears, where the water was coming from. Bobby was breathing hard, looking straight ahead as we drove the bumpy ranch roads.

"Marion's a stupid girl. You can't fuck around with teeth. She's too old. It won't grow back. I know what she was doing, and it doesn't work if you have a rotten heart. They're connected to your brain, too, your teeth, how you process pain, how you remember. Feel your teeth, how far up in your head they go?"

I ran my tongue across my gums.

"All calcium," he said.

He put his hand on my back and rubbed my bare skin up and down.

"And this, what you have here—we all used to be fish. Your spine's what's left of those aquatic skeletons."

I closed my eyes, imagining horrible fish swimming through murky, primordial waters. He told me then how the symbols were gathering around him, how it had to do with me coming into their lives, with the dreams he had of the floors of his childhood home covered with white figs, with the number of times he had found a dead deer on the ranch. His bees were disappearing, entire colonies collapsing for no reason. He found them in piles, their furred legs covered with dust and pollen. He could feel it, he said, a thrumming in the trees and all around, could feel that things were falling apart from the inside. Tonight confirmed it. He told me I shouldn't worry, that I was a light-holder and that things would be fine and that I would have to stay away for a little while. Marion would call me soon, he said. We could be friends again, but I knew it wasn't true.

"You're a sweet girl," he said, his hand on my shoulder. "You're better than all of them."

MACK THE KNIFE

HE HAD BEEN SAD, CLINICALLY SO, but overall things had improved. It was spring. Jonathan was no longer on certain medications: his headaches had gotten better, he slept through the night. The evening was a nice one, warm enough for a T-shirt. He'd bought five identical ones, fairly expensive, in a rush of optimism. Now he worried that they were maybe too tight. On the way to dinner, Jonathan dropped off Annie's homework folder at his ex-wife's building. He left it with the doorman; Maren had asked that he stop coming upstairs.

—

HARTWELL HAD PICKED the restaurant; he was the only one of the three who cared enough to have an opinion. Paul and Jonathan would have been happy getting a mediocre burger at one of the old standbys, unchanged from their youth. The restaurant on Great Jones was newer, busy even on a Monday night. They had a corner table. Hartwell looked around happily—pleased, Jonathan assumed, with the sense of being a part of things, tapped into some invisible current of city living. It was unspoken that they would all get drunk. The waitress was young but not attractive. That didn't seem to matter. She played at flirting with them, they played at flirting back.

"We've got to get the crispy squid, right?" Hartwell asked. "You like it?"

"It's fantastic," she said.

Hartwell ordered the squid, as if this was a personal favor to the waitress. When she walked away, Jonathan could sense that Hartwell was almost about to say something about the waitress, but didn't. In addition to the squid, a platter of shrimp and oysters, clams, a rib eye for two that the three of them would share, crusty with pepper. A side of broccoli rabe that no one would touch. They took turns sawing at the steak on a large wooden board in the middle of the table. Jonathan flagged down the waitress to order fries. It had been almost two months since they'd all managed to see each other. Paul's son was waiting to hear back from colleges.

"He wants to go west," Paul said. "Which would be pretty great, though who knows."

His son was a sweet kid, like Paul, though both of them shared that blinkered quality, as if life had stunned them. Since his son's hospitalization, Paul had taken to wearing a necklace, a single blue bead on a cord. It was getting a little grimy, the cord a little gray. Jonathan would have made fun of it under different circumstances. They'd known each other since they were toddlers. Strange how Paul could be both the fifty-year-old man and then shift, there, the thirteen-year-old boy who was the tallest of all of them, the most handsome, some golden light on him. Paul's son's cancer had gone into remission, but Jonathan had heard from Hartwell's wife that the long-term prognosis was not good.

Jonathan and Paul had never spoken about this directly.

At the most recent party Jonathan hosted, attended mostly by Julia's friends, Paul had been one of the last to leave. He'd done a line of coke with Julia and her manager, then followed Jonathan around, wanting to talk, even as Jonathan puttered and cleaned, emptying the ashtrays into the garbage, dumping the dregs from plastic cups down the sink. They should bicycle the French wine country, Paul said. Or why not do some of the Pacific Crest Trail? Or all of it? Hadn't they always talked about that, in college? Paul had an idea for a TV show he wanted Jonathan to write. Jonathan would, they both understood, never write this show. Neither of them would ever hike any portion of the Pacific Crest Trail. They weren't those kind of people.

In the fall, when Julia had left him, Paul had called Jonathan nearly every day, checking up on him. Remembering this made Jonathan, sitting with his old friends, feel like crying. He knew that Paul loved him. Across the table, Hartwell laughed open-mouthed, pushing his glasses up his face. Paul hacking ineffectually at the rib eye.

A text from Julia. He checked his phone under the table. She was having drinks with a friend who lived in her neighborhood, some guy named Kito. He was a nice guy, claimed to have watched and even enjoyed some of Jonathan's shows, though Jonathan's scripts were often doctored until his original idea had been wholly erased. He used to make jokes about the ship of Theseus, back when he cared more about people thinking he was smart. Now he mostly wanted people not to think about him at all.

Still with Kito, say hi to harts etc

Will do, Jonathan texted back.

"Julia says hi," he announced.

"Does she want to come meet us for dessert?" Hartwell said. "Or we could get another round somewhere else?"

"That's okay, she's in Gowanus with her friend," Jonathan said. "She actually met Ted last week."

They'd had a six P.M. dinner with his father at one of the relentlessly stolid restaurants in

Midtown, big blowsy light fixtures made of draped silk, a cheesy maître-d' with Dentyne breath by the coat check. Julia had changed twice, ended up in expensive plaid pants he had bought for her that she'd never worn before and one of his old wool sweaters. "I feel like a newsie," she said.

"Did she love Ted?" Hartwell said.

Hartwell was the only person Jonathan knew who actually did love Jonathan's father. Ted hosted Hartwell's entire family for an Easter weekend at the Millbrook house, Hartwell and his sporty wife, his weirdo kids. It irritated Jonathan, how tolerant his father seemed of Hartwell's kids, even Jax, Hartwell's youngest boy, a drama queen who wore what Jonathan was pretty sure were girl's leggings, kept announcing the Mandarin word for every object in sight. Ted had merely nodded along agreeably.

Hartwell and Jonathan walked down to the lake to smoke his vape pen before dinner, came back enjoyably stoned, which had been great until the ham on their plates took on some freaky cast of human flesh. Afterward, Hartwell had written a thank-you note that his father still mentioned in almost every conversation. Since his mother had died, his father had grown sentimental, newly touched by such gestures.

"Doubtful," Jonathan said. "No love between them. Maybe like." His father had been on edge at dinner, talked helplessly about the renovation, stared too long at the server when she asked if he was truly finished with the cioppino. It had surprised him that his father even knew what cioppino was—anything vaguely European used to agitate him. There had been some lulls, some silences, Julia drank too much. Jonathan too tired to really run interference. Hard to imagine his father didn't immediately run to his brothers with gossip about Jonathan's young girlfriend, barely past thirty. Or, worse, talked to Maren. Apparently they were still in touch, another development that shocked Jonathan. He only found out after Maren mentioned it during drop-off.

"You're brave, pal," Hartwell said. "I'm sure it was fine."

"We'll see."

The waitress came back with another round

of drinks, though Jonathan had already had one drink too many; two bourbons, now this second beer. He wished he hadn't quit smoking. This was the part of the night where he might step out for a quick cigarette, drunk enough to feel all was well, that he had good friends, that he hadn't misunderstood the basic rules, hadn't ended up in a dark wood. But no more smoking, no more high-cholesterol foods, or at least he was supposed to eat less of them. According to Julia. For reasons of longevity.

There was a very famous artist in his sixties who lived in Jonathan's building with his wife; she was thirty years younger, now pregnant with their third child. Jonathan often passed the artist smoking on the sidewalk in front of the building, smoking furiously, viciously, as if to hurry along death, and occasionally Jonathan ran into him in the elevator, the artist carrying his toddler in his arms, ignoring the kid's relentless punches. Jonathan knew they had a few industry friends in common, but they'd never spoken to each other. He seemed to be, sometimes, an auger of the unhappy future in store for Jonathan—how foolish the artist looked, gray-haired, jawline blurry, carrying his young child. He looked like a gruesome old man. Once Jonathan had seen the artist with his head buried in his hands, leaning against the window of the antique store on the building's ground floor. Jonathan couldn't tell if he was crying.

"Do we get dessert?" Hartwell asked.

It was a pointless question: Hartwell always got dessert. Blood orange granita, sticky toffee pudding with bourbon maple ice cream. Paul scooped up bites of ice cream with a nice buzzy smile. Sweet Paul. Hartwell was telling them about some historic tree at his country house that had been resuscitated via a Japanese landscaping technique that used other tree branches.

"No nails," he said. "They cut notches, slot it all together. Pretty beautiful."

He'd hired a Master Gardener. God knows where he heard of these things. Right after Jonathan separated, when he was still in the habit of sneaking around, Hartwell let him and Julia use the house for a weekend. They stood at the island to eat shrimp cocktail out of a plastic takeout container, watched half of a movie. They smoked a little weed from a metal vaporizer. Jonathan enjoyed cleaning the device with pipe cleaners sold especially for that purpose. Julia used a weed delivery service that only sold to women, and all the delivery people were women—inordinately and needlessly beautiful women. At first he wasn't sure if he could be in Julia's apartment when they came. Like you had to avoid any taint of men. But they didn't seem to mind, or no one said if they did. The fact of a stranger in the apartment, a beautiful woman, made the situation automatically erotic, the first scene of a porno. But all of them seemed aware of this trope, and as a result, they were archly, relentlessly professional. Even so, Jonathan was always deflated, when the women left, disappointed that nothing had happened, though it was impossible for him to see how anything would happen, to even conceive of what a possible first step would look like.

WITHOUT DISCUSSING IT, HARTWELL paid the check. Hartwell had loaned Jonathan a significant amount of money; this was another thing that was never spoken of.

"Hey, thanks," Jonathan said. "I'll get the next one." Did he sound convincing?

"No worries," Hartwell said, signing the receipt, folding the copy neatly and slipping it into his wallet. "Up for another drink?"

Jonathan checked his phone. Julia had called. Then texted multiple times over the last hour.

Kito gave me ketamine should I do?

lol bad idea or no?

Going to.

Come over

Where u

Where r u

He couldn't tell whether she was joking or not.

"Julia says she has ketamine."

"Really?"

Jonathan shrugged. He was going to make a joke about his druggy juvenile delinquent girlfriend, though Julia was, in fact, nearly thirty-two. Sometimes he caught himself making jokes about her for no real reason.

"I'm curious what it's like."

"Never done it," said Paul.

"They're starting to prescribe it. I read an article. I think it's FDA approved."

"I wonder if insurance would cover it," Hartwell said.

Strange how the furtive drug-taking of their childhoods had morphed into a kind of hobby, perfectly acceptable, like an interest in wine or coffee. One of his college friends invested in a dispensary in New Jersey. Hartwell's boss microdosed. It made it all a little less fun. They were basically responsible people. They'd had too much to drink but would be in bed by eleven.

Paul cleared his throat, pushed his chair back. "I should go," he said. "Make sure she doesn't kill herself."

PAUL LIVED IN BROOKLYN, so he and Jonathan walked toward the subway in companionable silence. Taking the train instead of a cab made Jonathan feel virtuous, on top of things. He was being responsible, wasn't he? Before they'd left, the waitress had brought them each a cellophane bag of tiny chocolate muffins, rocky with oats and nuts. "For your breakfast tomorrow," she said. Hartwell had all but waggled his eyebrows. "Thanks, Samantha," he said, putting an emphasis on the waitress's name. The waitress smiled back but already her eyes were scanning the room. She would forget about them in exactly one second.

JONATHAN OPENED THE BAG of tiny muffins on the sidewalk, tearing the sticker with the restaurant's logo. He was drunk enough to eat the whole bag without really knowing that he was. The streets were busy, girls tugging down the hems of summer dresses they'd worn for the first warm day and now regretted. He noticed these new headphones that everyone suddenly had, headphones without cords—they looked, to Jonathan, like some kind of medical device, stents to drain brain fluid. He would likely end up buying a pair, even so, because that seemed to be how things happened, like his eleven-year-old with her iPhone, though he had sworn such a thing would never be. At least Annie played spelling games, he told himself, though lately she'd become obsessed with some gothy game that required the constant purchase of gems. Julia played sometimes when she couldn't sleep—she'd gotten strangely good, stabbing the screen with a finger, her face glowing in the reflected light of a gently pulsing forest.

They were almost to the subway when Jonathan saw a cab approach. He stepped out into the street, raised an arm.

"Why not, right?" he said. "It's late."

"Sure," Paul said, "works for me."

"Two stops," Jonathan said, leaning in.

So he hadn't taken the subway, but at least he'd intended to. And certain taxi rides at night across the bridge seemed like shortcuts to feeling good about living in the city. You could imagine they were almost true, all the things you once believed about adulthood.

"Hard to believe it's already May," Paul said. "Basically summer."

"You guys going to Millbrook?"

"Annie's in camp for August. Maybe Julia and I will rent out East for some of it."

It was a nice thought, but unlikely. He

didn't have the money for a house out there. He and Julia had gone to the beach last summer, brought a Ziploc bag filled with cherries and ice, a container of green olives, and a bottle of warm seltzer. They'd finished all the snacks on the car ride. She was a terrible swimmer even though she'd grown up on the coast of Washington State—no one swam in the ocean there, it was too cold. She wouldn't go out past where she could touch. She worried about sand in her suit, she worried about salt water in her contacts. She pinched her nose shut every time she went under a wave. "I love this," she said, and he saw in her sunburned face that she legitimately did. She kicked away a float of algae coming toward her. "It makes you feel like a good human."

"We used to play Dead Bodies," he told her, "when we were kids. This game. We made it up. You sit where the wave breaks and the rule is you can't use your hands."

"So you just get knocked around? That's a horrible game."

"It was fun," he said, and it was—the rush of helplessness, danger that was both real and not real. Paul had been the best ocean swimmer in their group of friends by far—he was the best at everything. The first to have sex, the first to do hard drugs, the first to swim out past the buoys at camp. He'd always seemed like a man, the rest of them still boys, maybe forever.

Jonathan wanted to ask Paul if he remembered playing Dead Bodies, but Paul's eyes were closed, his arms crossed over his chest. The rush of air and noise from the open windows made it easy for Jonathan to close his eyes, too.

When the taxi stopped on Paul's corner, Paul patted his pockets. "I'll give you a twenty?"

"It's fine," Jonathan said, waving him away. "I got it." A queasy thought, but maybe true—these feelings of generosity just hid the part of him that wanted to keep someone around whose suffering was reliably greater than his own. Maybe Hartwell felt that way about Jonathan.

"Well, thanks, Johnny." Paul was the only person who still called him that. "See you soon?"

"Yeah. Yes. Say hi to Wendy."

—

ANOTHER TEN MINUTES OR SO in the cab till he hit Julia's neighborhood. His father had likely never been to Brooklyn. Jonathan took his daughter here, once, when he was still married—Annie seemed confused as to why they were in this neighborhood, why they'd taken a train ride just to get ice cream and walk by a dirty river. Still, she was young enough to be amiable, to trust in some overarching logic behind the things he did. They got hamburgers and hot dogs and she held the beeper the cashier gave them like it was a cellphone and mimed taking pictures of herself.

Love you he texted Annie, even though she was asleep. She'd shown him once how to text a pulsing heart but he couldn't remember how. Annie genuinely made him laugh. Sometimes it worried him to see the desperation edging her manic jokes, but maybe that was just projection. She was certainly sturdier than he had ever been, less wounded. Even in childhood photos of himself, Jonathan thought the portent of future despair was somehow visible, a tendency toward miscalculation.

Once, while fumbling for a story for Julia, he'd told her about the baby squirrel, Snoopy, that he and his nanny had rescued from Central Park when Jonathan was six. It was strange that his parents had indulged this, but they had, Jonathan feeding the squirrel with sugar water, petting him with one finger, ferrying the tiny animal in a shoebox in his lap from Eightieth Street to Millbrook every weekend. After a while, his mother announced it was time to bring Snoopy back to the wild. She'd taken Jonathan to the park, pointed out all the other squirrels, all the trees for Snoopy to climb. Jonathan didn't remember whether he was sad, leaving his pet behind, only that his mother had rushed them away as soon as the other squirrels circled Snoopy, lunging and shrieking. It wasn't Snoopy, it was some other one they were attacking, his mother told him as they walked back to the apartment. It only occurred to Jonathan, as he was telling Julia the story, that of course the other squirrels had killed Snoopy. Why had he never realized that before? They could sense something soft in Snoopy, something unfit for the world, too many hours in an old Bass Weejun shoebox on the Taconic, too much needless, grasping love from a six-year-old who was afraid of everything; darkness, moths, his older brothers. When he told Julia the story, she teared up but was laughing at the same time. Why did it make her sad? She imagined the squirrel would greet him in heaven, that Snoopy would somehow be tasked with spiriting him to the next world. She was both joking and not.

JONATHAN GOT OUT AT the corner so the cab wouldn't have to circle around. Julia didn't answer his call. He walked in the direction of her apartment, called again. It still felt new to be back in her neighborhood, the six months that they were broken up long enough to estrange most everything. She had dated a co-star on her show—he was basically her age. Jonathan texted when he heard her show had been unexpectedly canceled, but she didn't text back. He only found out later that she'd been living with this new person. They didn't talk about it. Jonathan dated someone, too, a woman in her forties with two kids, an administrator at a performing arts high school. Isabel was kind, interesting, endlessly accommodating. She had a dark bob and a low, appealing voice. They sent photos of their children back and forth. She texted in full sentences and with assiduous attention to grammar. After they'd kissed the first time, she'd smiled sweetly to herself, privately. Jonathan could see her resist the idea of being together, foreseeing some future pain, and then allow herself to move forward anyway. They ordered Thai food and watched actual movies, went to the dog run with her Australian shepherd. In every way, Isabel had seemed the correct person. Even breaking up with her had been easy—she made him feel he was being somehow honorable. Why hadn't he told Julia about Isabel? When he was still married he would sometimes lie to Maren about small things: what he had eaten for lunch, what time he'd gone to sleep. It was pointless, harmless, except that it made him comfortable with the idea that reality was mutable.

—

IT WAS BETTER FOR him and Julia to focus on the salient points. They were back together. Jonathan was officially divorced. There were no more limitations to rear up against, no background music of unfairness or tragedy. Julia had gotten what she wanted, or maybe what she had started to believe she wanted. Hard not to go along with the prevailing story, the cliché—she wanted him to leave his wife, he did not, and so on, and everyone played their part correctly. Sometimes on those old phone calls he could hear her lines before she said them, like they were being fed to her offstage: "You said you loved me. You made a promise."

Julia was depressed. Julia picked fights, or maybe he did, it was hard to tell. Lately after their fights he would lie in the darkness with his phone and scroll through old texts from Isabel, meaning to send a message, see how she was doing. He never did. It would be too disrupting, too much like the old days, how one minute his life was a cohesive thing, knowable, and then suddenly it was alien, uncanny, still recognizable but changed in a fundamental way. Was the rebuilt ship still the same ship? He tried to explain it to Julia once, the stupid Theseus's ship thing. She barely listened. And who cared about the moment an old boat became the new boat? Maybe the real problem was that you couldn't ever make something different, that you couldn't make, say, a house. Even if you replaced all your shitty old boards with new boards and really believed you might end up somewhere new, really believed you might be making a house—even then, after all that work, you still had a boat. He had changed so much, changed everything. So it was worse, then, to look up, the dust settled, and see his life taking the same old shape.

Occasionally he missed the antidepressants.

He called Julia again and she finally picked up.

"Hi."

Her voice sounded strange.

"You okay?"

"I'm on drugs," she said, then laughed. "I need you."

"I'm a block away."

—

HE COULD SEE HER LIGHT was on from the street. Her buzzer didn't work, so he texted her again. After what seemed like a long time, he saw movement. Through the window of the front door he watched her make her way down the stairs. She gripped the banister. Her eyes were very wide. She wouldn't look at him, opening the second door, reaching up to unlock the deadbolt. Her hand hovered above the lock without moving—she looked, from the darkness outside, quite frightened. But when she actually got the door open, she smiled at him, big, bringing him into the light. She was wearing a long-sleeve T-shirt and her striped underwear.

"Hello." She kept smiling, blinking.

He laughed a little. "You were serious."

"Let's go upstairs," she said.

On the last flight of steps, she sank in slow motion to her knees. She smiled at him. "I'll get up," she said. He pulled her to her feet.

"Jesus," he said, but it was funny. She seemed fine. He already imagined telling Hartwell this story tomorrow.

The lightbulb was out on her landing; he could make out piles of boxes, flattened and tied with twine, empty storage bins. A bicycle with two flat tires. Her many winter coats humped over a rack.

"Dirty," she said, pushing open the door.

Her apartment was dark except for a floor lamp, one of her little cheapo lamps on the nightstand. So much garbage everywhere. Amazon boxes, half-unpacked plastic bags from the pharmacy, dying plants. Her manager had been sending orchids—a comically fussy present to give to someone who was depressed, struggling with basic tasks. She didn't read scripts anymore, either. These were bundled outside with the boxes. Some of the plastic bags were filled with empty water bottles waiting to be brought to the recycling downstairs. Wouldn't it be easier for her to just get a water filter? He'd stopped trying to fix what seemed to him like solvable problems—maybe she didn't want things to be easier.

—

WHEN JULIA WAS WAITING to hear about an audition, she used to wake up in the mornings, frozen, unable to really speak. He would blink awake to see her bare back, turned from him, and he'd lay a hand on her, sometimes moving his hand in circles. Only many months later did he realize these were panic attacks. By the time he understood this, they'd mostly stopped. She'd taken mood stabilizers but quit two weeks ago. Hard to tell if she was doing better. He could feel Julia tracking his concern for her and that his concern made her anxious. He had her sister's phone number in case things got bad again. So far, so good. Things were normalizing. He still went into other rooms to talk to his daughter on the phone. Sometimes Julia was watching a TV show on his iPad and a FaceTime call would appear, his ex-wife's smiling photo sudden in the frame. Julia dropped the iPad on instinct, as if she might somehow be visible. They were used to secrets, he supposed, all of them, a life lived parallel to real life. But now this was real life. He had to remind himself of that.

—

"COME TO BED," JULIA SAID, "I have to lie down." She got under the comforter. Her laptop was open at half-mast, a folky song playing through the tiny speakers. The ceiling fan was going. "Are you listening?" she said. "I love this." Her words were slurred and mild. "It's so pretty."

It was a cover—an old man singer he didn't recognize, but a song he knew.

"You know it's actually about a killer?" he said.

"Hm?"

"Yeah," he said. "If you listen, the words are legitimately scary."

"But it sounds so nice." She opened her eyes. "He gets growly there, it's good."

He took off his shoes, his pants. The song was a live recording, ending in applause. It began again.

"On repeat, I see," he said. She didn't respond.

They lay side by side, her hands clammy, her cold feet touching his ankles. When they first met, she'd never landed a real job. That had been years ago. She had a publicist now, a manager, though these days there was nothing for them to do.

She pointed at the nightstand. Among her prescriptions, her retinol, a protein bar wrapper, there was a little black scale, a clear plastic bag printed with Adidas logos.

"Slick," he said.

She smiled with her eyes closed.

"Very chic," she said, her voice petering out. "Kito didn't want it. I think you should do some."

He was drunk enough to feel happy lying there with her. Unconcerned. Nothing was wrong. She sometimes looked especially young, like she did that night. Her skin had evened out after a course of antibiotics, much to her delight. Her lips were very chapped. He loved her.

"You have to snort it?" he said.

She shrugged. "It's nice. It's weird." She kept opening her eyes as if suddenly jolted awake.

He checked his phone, got up to plug the charger into the wall. He took off his shirt, got back in bed. She studied his hand, rubbing her bare thigh in the dim room.

"I have asparagus legs," she said, making herself laugh.

"Oh really."

"Yes."

She lifted one leg and then the other, squinted at him.

"You're in the music video," she said. "Did you see it? You look like you're in the background with all the smoke, and the, what is it, ladders. Scaffolding."

She sat up with great effort. "Wow," she said. "You do it."

She balanced the electronic scale on a book, narrowing her eyes at the buttons.

"I'm going to do more, too," she said, "but just a little."

She tipped out white flakes onto the scale. The numbers blinked and reset.

"Very professional," he said. "How much are you supposed to take?"

"I actually," she said, "don't know, the scale doesn't work. But it was. It did."

She snorted half a line through a loosely rolled dollar bill.

"Yuck," he said.

"I make you one," she said. "It's really not bad for you, you can't die or anything."

Did she sound slightly manic?

He took the bill from her to reroll it more tightly. In college, he had a little cocaine problem. Had even been famous on campus for the prodigious amounts he could take down in a night. Not much else to do in the New Hampshire woods, there with the same kinds of people he'd grown up with and gone to high school with, the unchanging cast of his whole life. That year in college had probably been the only time until the divorce that he'd actually done anything wrong, made choices that felt even a bit dangerous. And maybe it had even been disappointing how quickly that period had passed, how there had, really, been no consequences. A semester off to travel, to cool it with the drugs, but that was it. He graduated on time, was herded into the predictable grooves of his adult life. It was almost like nothing had ever happened.

The song had played a few times through. "Children of the darkness. I like it."

She was lying down again. He touched her thigh, her crotch through her underwear. She didn't respond.

"What's your shirt?" It was cluttered with black-and-white graphics, a sun, a pair of dice, a grainy photograph. It was unusual for her.

"Do you like it?"

"Sure."

She stretched out her arms to study the shirt. "So you like it?"

"What?"

"My shirt."

He rolled his eyes. "Yes."

"I should take my contacts out."

Together they blinked up at the ceiling fan.

"Can we listen to something else?" he said.

She muted her computer. "Okay." She clicked around the trackpad with one limp finger. "You'll do some, right? You'll like it."

He was ridiculous, a ridiculous old man doing drugs. "Sure," he said. He didn't have his daughter till Friday. There was nothing that desperately needed to get done anytime soon, just notes on a show he no longer cared about, a show that would likely never get made. At a certain point, you stopped hoping things got made and started wishing for kill fees.

"You need anything? I'm getting us water."

She didn't answer.

HER KITCHEN WAS TINY. More of a corner, really. Her freezer had been left ajar, emitting a breath of chilly light. He shut it. Julia had taken out a fresh trash bag but only draped it on the lid of the garbage can. He would fix all this in the morning, take the recycling downstairs, maybe try to get a lightbulb for the hallway. He drank a glass of water, looking out into the many dark yards of the neighbors, the city beyond the tops of the brownstones. It was a pleasing scene, the lights of the tall buildings in the distance and the human scale of the apartments. He rinsed the glass and left it dripping on the dish rack.

WHEN HE RETURNED TO the bedroom, he saw Julia's eyes were filled with tears. "Gee," she said, her voice mawkish, "but I'm not really sad." She looked scared. He petted her hair, took the scale from her and put it on the nightstand. Tears fell down her cheek, running into her hair. "It's okay," she said.

It hurt him, suddenly, to see it. How plain it was—she was trying so very hard. Still waiting to find out whether this would turn out to be a bad story or a good one. He used to visit her in her old apartment. It was a time when he would bring her things he thought she'd like: tins of pastilles, books, a cardigan the color of a grapefruit. Her bed was lofted, close to the ceiling. It was summer and there were occasionally silverfish skittering into the corners. He ordered her silverfish repellent off Amazon, bought her a window unit when July rolled around, though he wasn't there to help her install it. It made him feel collegiate to have sex in a bed you had to climb a ladder to get to. She'd been taking sleeping meds then and used to call him with weird hallucinations, a dark cloaked figure waiting at the bottom of the ladder, urging her to roll out of bed. "It made sense 'cause I was so afraid of accidentally falling out," she'd said. "I was so afraid and I just wanted it to happen. So then

I could just do it and stop being afraid it was going to happen." He remembered that time fondly, though this was the period of their relationship she seemed to bring up most often in fights. Crying so hard she was gasping—you left me alone, she would say. You left me.

"MAYBE WE CAN SPEND some time at the beach this summer," he said. "You liked it."

Julia was breathing softly. Her face was wet but she had stopped crying. She put on some classical music: it surprised him she even had it on her computer.

"Remember?" he said. "We'll play Dead Bodies."

"Dead Bodies," she said.

"It'll be great. I'll teach you to swim in the ocean." As he said the words, he believed them. In truth he was not a strong swimmer.

She opened her eyes but didn't say anything, just watched him. He bent over the scale and snorted the line. She hadn't crushed it fine enough. Maybe this had been dumb. He dipped down and finished it.

"You won't even feel anything in the morning," she said.

They had gotten everything they wanted.

"Because it's very pure," she said, "one of the thirty pure drugs in the world."

Then she laughed, her eyes closed. "What am I even talking about."

A/S/L

MOUNTAIN, MOUNTAIN, MOUNTAIN. Mountains on every side. Mountains that looked pixelated by gravel and chaparral, mountains that looked like their faces were crumbling. At certain hours of the day, with the sun disappeared and the mountains outlined, the mountain range looked like a tidal wave, about to crash down, about to sweep everything clean.

THE STEADY DESERT HEAT meant Thora applied and reapplied medicated lip balm, refilled her water bottle from communal jugs, water tinted by lemon slices and mint.

They weren't allowed cellphones but could call home as much as they liked—after the first week, anyway. They could go into town with staff supervision. Thora didn't leave the Center, but her roommate, Ally, came back with turquoise dream catchers and magazines, big Saran-wrapped cookies from the bakery.

When Thora wasn't in group, or doing check-ins with her counselor, she and Ally sat out by the pool in terrycloth robes, on lounge chairs that smelled a little moldy. Ally was twenty, the daughter of a senator. She wondered aloud how many Instagram followers she might have lost without her phone. Because Ally had diabetes, the staff let her keep her insulin and syringes, which she carried around in a pink zip purse with a crown on it.

Keep Calm and Carry On.

Thora liked to watch Ally inject herself, pooch up the pale skin above her waistband. It was almost like doing drugs herself.

All in all, it was a nice place. The landscaping was professional, attended to by many sunburned men. The food had a prechewed quality, lots of purees and smoothies, though, famously, the meals were good, better than at other places. Thora could attest to that, no soggy chicken fingers, no frozen chocolate cake crispy with ice shards. They were well nourished. The staff gave out vitamins in plastic organizers, grainy vitamins, probiotics in chocolate form, which was another way to tell this was not quite rehab but some way station before rehab, the rules loosely enforced, the idea of authority introduced without the necessary follow-through.

It was more of a holding pen, a quiet place—it was assumed that everyone there was very tired. They were all overworked, stressed, and perhaps that had led them to make bad decisions that had adversely affected the people around them. The Media Room was stacked with old Academy screeners, though every night for the last two weeks, Ally and Thora watched a Ken Burns documentary about national parks. This alone seemed to take years off their lives.

WHEN THORA CALLED JAMES, once a day, she could tell he was summoning a sort of gravitas, performing a solemnity he would later report to his therapist. He was attempting, she realized, to be present. Thora had only been gone two weeks: already James had started to seem theoretical, a series of still photos that didn't quite coalesce into someone she had married.

"You sound strong," James said. "Really."

"Mm," Thora said.

"I love you," James said, somber, his voice dropped an octave.

For a moment, she studied the silence between them with curiosity: suddenly she could do things like this, stop answering, stop talking, and it was fine.

She forced herself to speak. "I love you, too."

James was, she knew, not a bad person.

THEY WERE BORED, lights out, Thora's headlamp illuminating the corners of the room: the not-terrible abstract paintings, the window cracked to let in the night air. Outside were the dark shapes of the big aloe plants, the cacti. Thora stared at the twin beds, the matching coverlets. She hadn't shared a room since college. It had been so long ago: she couldn't remember if she'd actually liked any of her friends, the girl she lived with who kept her hair short, who baked loaves of sourdough in the dorm kitchen. She was a wilderness guide now. Thora was sure her life would seem appalling to the girl. Maybe it was.

Ally slept naked. Thora could've complained about this, she guessed—complaints were almost encouraged, showed they were setting limits and responding proactively to their environments—but she didn't care. Thora liked the blunt fact of Ally's presence, liked watching Ally move around, inspecting one of her pale tits for nipple hair under the lamplight. They took away Ally's tweezers after she plucked every hair from her left armpit, though she showed Thora she could do it with her fingernails, too. She often fell asleep with one hand on her crotch, as if it was a pet. That night, Ally was absorbed in the book she'd been reading the last two weeks. Thora had seen a lot of people carrying the book around the Center: making a big deal of bringing it to lunch, women squeezing the hardcover tightly to their chests as they walked to Restorative Yoga.

"Can I see?" Thora said. Ally passed it over.

Thora read just a few pages. It was about a plucky dollmaker in occupied Paris during World War II. It seemed like a book for people who hated books.

"This is terrible," Thora said, flipping the book to see the author photo. A woman stared back from a razzle of Aztec jewelry. "The author looks like the world's most cheerful nine-year-old."

"It's actually really good," Ally said, snatching it back. Thora had hurt her feelings.

"Sorry," Thora said. Ally didn't respond, on the edge of pouting. She pulled the covers up over herself, turning away from Thora.

"Wanna test my blood?" Thora said.

At this, Ally brightened. She sat up. She had been begging Thora to let her test her blood sugar.

"Come here," she said, patting her bed, taking out her little pink purse. Suddenly she seemed very professional, despite her nudity.

Ally held Thora's right hand in hers, palm up, the fingers splayed.

"Here we go."

Ally jabbed Thora's finger, then held a piece of paper to absorb the drop of red. It stung worse than she had imagined it might. Thora sucked her fingertip hard.

"You do this to yourself all the time?"

"One-oh-five," Ally said, briskly, after feeding the paper slip into her little machine. "Very nice."

Ally dropped the used needle into an empty seltzer bottle, a poky mess of trash and bloody napkins that she kept on her nightstand, like a gory snow globe.

THORA WOKE IN THE blue morning light, Ally's voice coming from the bed next to her. "The people are eating," she muttered. "The people are eating." The medication Ally was taking seemed to make her a little crazy. When Thora went to check on her, she saw Ally was still asleep, a pillow clenched between her knees.

"You just kept repeating yourself," Thora told her at breakfast. "Over and over."

Ally pushed for details, asking Thora

whether she'd said anything else. "I can handle it," she said, "just tell me," and it struck Thora that Ally wasn't nervously patrolling the spill of her psyche, worried about what poisonous things she'd let slip, but that Ally genuinely hoped to learn something valuable and unknown about herself.

BEFORE SHE'D COME HERE, Thora had gotten in what her counselor Melanie would call a bad spiral.

It was the afternoons that did it, three o'clock like a kind of death knell, the house seeming too still, too many hours of sunlight left in the day. How had Thora even started going to the chatrooms? The last time she had been in a chatroom was in high school, sleepovers where girls crowded around a desktop computer and wrote sickening things to men, all of it a joke, then furtively masturbated in their sleeping bags. Or at least Thora had. And now she was back, typing in a username.

Thora18.

How quickly the messages had come in:

Hey Thora!
Cute name
Asl
Asl
Wanna chat
Asl?
Are you 18 or 18 isshhh ☺

It amused her, on her laptop in bed, her husband at work, to reply to these men. To conjure an eighteen-year-old that did not exist, an eighteen-year-old that Thora had never been, certainly: blond, blue-eyed, a member of the cheerleading squad. Did high schools still have cheerleading squads? It didn't matter how ridiculous the things she said were, how big she made her tits, how short she made the skirt of her supposed cheer uniform, the men seemed to believe, wholeheartedly, that she was real. A ludicrous illusion they were building together, and she found she enjoyed the back-and-forth. Pretending not to know why the men were chatting with her. Writing **hahahaha** whenever they brought up sex. **What's that,** she typed when someone mentioned double penetration. When they asked her pointed, leading questions about her **real** age, she finally agreed that she was, in fact, only sixteen.

They were ecstatic, writing back instantly, the sudden use of exclamation points like cardiograms from their throbbing erections:

I won't tell babe don't worry!!!!

Her stupidity delighted these men. They had found her, at last: a teen cheerleader who wanted to learn about sex, who wanted to learn about it from them! Too stupid to understand what they were taking from her!

After a while they wanted photos. She ignored the requests, usually, closing the window, but then she thought, why not?

She spent a good hour on the bed, trying to take a photo with her face mostly hidden, a photo where she didn't look thirty-five but instead looked like a teenager: a finger in her mouth, her tongue peeping out like a little cat. Her tongue looked strange, too pale, but if she used a filter, one arm covering her nipples, she might look eighteen.

The men loved the photo. But then they wanted more.

Are you shaved?

Oh ya, she said. She was not.

How many dicks have you seen.

Um, she would type. **2. Is that weird?**

Have you ever had a boyfriend?

No, she typed. **I wisshhhhhh!**

Amazing how this ate up the afternoon, four hours passing without Thora looking up from the screen. She had missed two texts from James.

If she had better friends, she would have told them about what she was doing. Or if James was a different kind of person. Because wasn't it sort of funny? She had an entire run of photos of herself on her phone now: bending over, the seat of her underwear pulled tightly across her ass, pictures of her face from the nose down, a nipple between her fingers. They all wanted a pussy shot: she found one off the Internet to use. She sent the same photo every time, so gradually she began to believe this bare pink pussy was her own pussy, and in fact began to feel proud of just how perfect this pussy—her pussy!—was.

She had never been the focus of so much attention. So many men trying to coax or trick her into giving them what they wanted. And that was the part she liked best, the knowing/unknowing—it wasn't possible to summon artificially, role-play wouldn't do it. It had to be real.

She only hated them when they got mean: when she told them she had to go, and they typed back, furious.

Are u fucking serious just help me cum pls

Pls

Im so hard

Bitch

When Thora got bored of talking to the same men, she started signing in under different names. Usually under **James45.** Sometimes **DaddyXO.** She talked with the men, pretended she was a man, too, and they sent her photos of teens in bikinis at public pools and she sent them photos of herself.

Such a whore, she typed. **Little teen whore.**

Mmmm fuck, a man typed back. **Love those teen tits.**

It seemed obvious that the photos of her were not photos of a teenager, but no matter.

Their wish that the tits belonged to a teenager was so strong that it created an alternate reality. She had never been so excited: seeing herself as these men did, some unformed idiot who needed to be fucked. Her sheets smelled like sweat, all the curtains drawn. She didn't eat for whole days.

"You're so wet," James said one night, surprised, when she put his hand in her underwear. But then they had sex the way they always did, James coming on her stomach, his body jerking in a series of convulsions, as though he were being riddled with bullets at the O.K. Corral.

It had all seemed funny except that, truly, she would rather do this than anything else: run the usual errands that kept things in motion, see James, have dinner with him. It was like having a calling, finally, the way she had once imagined she might. A life organized around a higher goal.

While James slept, his back turned to her and the covers kicked off, she typed furtively on her phone to men who sent photos of dicks, sometimes tiny squibs of flesh between massively fat thighs, sometimes overlarge penises with the porn watermark visible in the corner.

Wow, she always typed. **I don't know if it will fit.**

That was not the reason she had ended up at the Center, exactly, the chats, but it hadn't helped.

THERE WAS A HIKE in the morning, before the temperatures got unbearable. On the drive to the trailhead, Melanie had turned the radio to a Christian talk station Thora mistook for NPR until they said "resurrection" one too many times.

Thora scrambled around the boulders, up through the dust and the sage. She drank lukewarm water; Melanie passed out protein bars. Last session, someone kept mashing these into coils and leaving them in the urinals, or so said Ally, a veteran of the program. It was a real problem, fake shit being essentially as difficult to clean as real shit. Was there a lesson there?

By the time they got back, G. had already arrived.

No one had known he was coming. He looked, if anything, exactly like the person in the newspaper photos—froggish, squashed, well fed. For all five seasons of his show, he had been clean-shaven, ruddy in his apron and concert T-shirts, big moony face damp with steam from whatever was cooking on the stove. Now he'd grown stubble, white, extending beyond his jawline to his neck and cheeks, giving his face the semblance of a shape. He wore a baseball hat and the same baggy clothes as the rest of them—sweatshirts, pants with soft waists. Their days were considered difficult enough that whatever energy they may have once expended on buttons and zippers was now worth diverting elsewhere.

Men and women were kept separate except for lunch, which most people ate in their rooms anyway. G., surprisingly, chose to eat at a shaded picnic table by the pool, close enough for Thora and Ally to study his froggy face for signs of evil, watch him pick at a sweet potato drowned in soy sauce.

Did he eat the sweet potato in a particularly evil way?

THE STAFF ALLOWED THEM their benzos and SSRIs as long as their home doctors kept the prescriptions current. Things like this made it hard to believe that anyone who worked there actually thought they were helping anyone. Ally and Thora sometimes swapped meds for fun; Thora took one dose of Ally's Lexapro and went into what felt like a light mania, pedaling the stationary bike for a solid hour, then eating ravenously, spilling salsa verde on her robe. The night that G. arrived, Ally took someone's Ambien but stayed awake, filling out her Dialectic Behavioral Workbook.

What are three concrete changes you can make in order to improve your life?

She showed Thora her answers the next morning, written in loopy Ambien scrawl:

1. **Buy puffy white sneakers**
2. **Double pierce my ears**
3. **Fuck G.**

Addled as she'd been on a sedative-hypnotic,

Ally brought up a good point: who was G. gonna fuck first?

G. WAS ASSIGNED ROBERT as his sober coach, tiny Robert who told everyone with pride that he had built the wood-fired pizza oven at the Center with his bare hands. "With the same clay the Mayans used," he said. No one asked any follow-up questions. Robert wore flip-flops, which seemed at odds with his desire for everyone to call him Coach.

Robert was appalled by their lives, in an exciting way—he'd worked for the government before, for institutions, so people having money the way people like them had money seemed to him like a cosmic joke. He tried to engage one of the business guys in an earnest debate about fracking, tried to explain the problems with a possible Bloomberg presidency. Thora would hear his voice from across the pool: "I can see where you're coming from, man, but have you ever considered—"

Robert stayed close to G.'s side, murmuring into his ear quietly enough so no one could make out what he was saying, though of course Thora and Ally tried their best, filled in the blanks, imagined all manner of foul behavior turned into a narrative, spun into a story of good and evil.

DURING THAT AFTERNOON'S phone hours, Thora called James. The phone room in the main building was busy, so she made the call in Robert's office, an adobe outbuilding on a concrete slab. Out front, there were half barrels on the porch where Robert was growing gray stalks of kale; a wind chime made of abalone shells hung from the eaves. His white dog was pregnant: she lurched heavily on her chain, then circled back to sit in the shade.

Thora's cheek was sweating where the phone was pressed to her ear.

"Does anyone even speak to him?" James asked. "Monster," he said, under his breath, though Thora could sense it, too—James was excited. They all were. Thora had read every disgusting thing G. had done: every hot-tub dick-graze, the Fleshlight in the greenroom, drugged-up gropes of cowering PAs in sensible flats. With his presence, the communal mood heightened a few degrees. The only other resident that conjured any frisson was a baseball player who'd been caught jacking off in an afternoon showing of **Despicable Me 3,** but that was nothing compared to G. Thora and Ally tracked G.'s every choice and activity, took any opportunity to smile at him or sit near him at meals. G. drank cucumber and kale juice in the morning. G. took Pilates from a private instructor in town. G. was trying to avoid nightshades after his food sensitivity test. G. appeared, to Thora's eye anyway, to have gone down a pants size.

"He keeps to himself," Thora said. "We're all just trying to do our best here."

There was a silence. She assumed they were both thinking of G.

"Well," James said. "I'm proud of you. Really."

Thora was on Focalin. Or had been, until they found out she had been snorting it off James's iPad, the iPad he loaded with podcasts about political crimes and interviews with precocious teens starting businesses. She'd tried listening to one of them once, one of James's beloved podcasts: when had life become so dull, an extended social studies class where you were supposed to summon interest in the workings of corporations, the minutiae of historical events, spend your free time cramming for a test that didn't exist?

Everyone was suddenly trying, so very hard, to learn things.

GROUP WAS KEPT SEPARATE by gender, and was supposedly confidential, another of the "rules" that turned out to be nothing more than a half-hearted suggestion: Russell told Ally and Thora everything from men's group when the three of them drank mugs of weedy chamomile out on the South Veranda.

"He cries almost every time," Russell said. Ally knew Russell from her last stay here, a year ago.

"No," Thora said.

"Truly. He doesn't get into it. But just says

he's here to learn. He knocked over my water bottle and apologized. Like, almost with tears in his eyes."

Ally leaned back on her elbows. "Probably fake tears."

"Robert doesn't even make him go into detail. Which is not exactly fair."

But G. didn't need to go into details, didn't need to unspool all the stories for the rest of them: they already knew everything. When Ally was asleep, Thora sometimes rubbed herself against her palm, imagining the bulk of G.'s body behind her, that belly, formidable from years of public gastronomy, slapping against her back. It only worked if she imagined G. believed he was taking something from her.

"Have you talked to him outside of group?"

"Nah," Russell said. "But guess what?" He was almost gleeful. "I have a UTI. My deek"—he pronounced it like that—"hurts," Russell said.

"I don't believe you," Ally said. "Guys don't get UTIs."

"Oh, it's for certain," he said. "The doctors

were surprised, too." Russell was proud in his insistence: blessed by rarity. His dick was like no other dick. And he did have a UTI. Thora had never heard of this happening before, but that's the way the spring had been going.

THE NEXT NIGHT, ALLY WAS reading her dollmaker book. Occasionally she pressed a hand to her heart, overcome. Russell had brought Thora a magazine from town, but she'd seen it already. A page of various celebrities with cellulite blurring their thighs. A different celebrity recording everything she ate in a day. Like all of them, around three P.M. the celebrity ate a handful of almonds as a snack. A cut-up bell pepper with hummus. Living that way seemed to require skills that Thora lacked. The ability to take your own life seriously, believing that you were a solid enough entity to require maintenance, as if any of it would add up to something.

She looked up from the magazine when there was movement on the sill.

"Shit," Thora said, "gross."

Ally glanced up from her book. Together they considered the moth on the sill, the dry feathery beast. It must have got in through the open window. The moth was sleeping, at least, its wings folded in prayerful repose.

"What should we do about it?"

"Just try to shoo it out the window?" Thora said.

Ally put down her book.

"Want to see something?" Ally said, unzipping her little pink purse, flicking her vial of insulin expertly. "We did this at diabetes camp once. No bubbles," she said, "that part is important." She got up on her knees, shuffling to the sill. "Are you watching?"

Thora rolled her eyes. "Yes."

Ally grasped the moth firmly between her fingers. It barely moved.

"Watch."

With impeccable swiftness, Ally injected the fat moth body with her insulin.

"What the fuck," Thora said. The moth spread its wings before starting to fly around the room, crazily.

They both shrieked. The moth slammed

into the wall and dropped dead. Ally, inexplicably, started laughing.

"Sick," she said.

ALLY AND THORA WERE G.'s most likely targets, the only ones in his preferred demographic. Most of the women at the Center were older—burned-out executives, plastic surgery recoveries, legit addicts who forestalled reality a little longer by wasting some soft money here, what amounted to a very expensive hotel stay. Thora studied herself in the bathroom mirror, picking the dead skin from her chapped lips. Would G. find her attractive? Ally was younger than Thora, which, historically, would have been a plus for G., but diabetes kept her pale, and her hair had gone a little green from the chlorine, her brows furring out without her tweezers.

Before lunch, Thora changed into a tight tank top, yoga pants that had a perverse seam in the crotch. She let her hair down at the picnic table, idly brushed it with her fingers over one shoulder. Ally was on some tear about how her father always told her she was beautiful and never **smart,** and wasn't that **sort of fucked up**? Thora wasn't paying attention: she was watching G., deep in conversation with Robert. He'd barely touched his stone-fruit Caprese.

G.'s daughter was definitely staying nearby. There were sightings. Russell had seen her on one of his excursions to town: Russell was desperate for mushrooms, trying to cadge some off the men with sunburned necks who rode BMX bikes along the main street, their bicycles evidence of suspended licenses from DUIs.

Later, Thora watched G. across the pool reading Robert's self-published book on accountability, pausing to balance it on his T-shirt-covered belly. Thora rubbed aloe sunscreen on her legs, slowly. Swimsuits weren't actually allowed by the pool except during gender-restricted swim hours—but no staff seemed to notice. But had G. noticed? Was G. going to come over? No, he was reaching for a pen, he was underlining something. When he got up, it was only to refill his water bottle, do a little yogic stretch, clasping his arms behind his back, straining his belly tight. In the last two days, he had started wearing a bracelet made of wooden beads around one wrist.

"Very **spiritual**," Russell said.

ROBERT'S DOG HAD FINALLY had her puppies: six squirming, mostly silent creatures with slitty eyes and little hamster claws. Robert plugged in a heating pad, nestled it among blankets in a cardboard box, though it was April, eighty degrees on Easter.

Robert set up the box in the common room. Thora assumed the puppies were meant to teach everyone about fragility, about caretaking. Ally held one to her chest, stroking it with a single finger.

"Tiny," Ally cooed. "Look at their little noses."

Thora held one, too. "So cute," she said, unconvincingly. When one of the puppies shit in the box, the mom ate it.

—

AT CHECK-IN, MELANIE ASKED if Thora was aware that she was wearing exercise clothes outside the gym area. She asked if Thora was aware that the dress code asks us not to expose our shoulders. Melanie asked Thora to

Scan her body
Assess her feelings
Locate the discomfort

What were her feelings? Mostly Thora felt drowsy—there in the carpeted room, the sun coming through the big windows.

Melanie wanted to talk about Thora's mood journal.

"If we can start to notice a pattern," Melanie said, "you'll be able to have a little more control."

There were dozens of plants behind Melanie, their glossy heart-shaped leaves twisting across the sill. Someone had to water them. Every week. The thought of anything needing regular care and upkeep suddenly made Thora even more tired. She crossed and uncrossed her legs. Melanie's cellphone rang.

"I can show you how to turn off the ringer,"

Thora said, when Melanie's phone rang for the third time. Did her voice sound as hateful as she felt? Melanie didn't respond. Melanie was looking at her with concern.

"I'll consider these questions in my journal," Thora said, finally.

Melanie both cared about Thora and did not really care—Thora saw Melanie's face toggle between these two absolutely true things.

AFTER BREAKFAST, RUSSELL, ALLY, and Thora saw G. and Robert leave for town. The huevos rancheros had solidified on Thora's plate, the beans now mortar. She'd eaten the fruit, enough to avoid a talk with Melanie, and Russell would likely finish the rest anyway. G.'s baseball cap was pulled low, his gait shuffly from his sandals. He paused to apply lip balm from a plastic sphere. No one knew why G. went into town so often, though maybe it was just to see his daughter. G. was working on a screenplay, they heard, or a memoir. Russell claimed to have shown him how to download Final Draft.

"But why is he allowed to have a laptop?"

Ally said. "If he tries to rape us, can we borrow his laptop?"

"Do we think he's going to jail?" Russell said.

Thora had read more about G. in the Business Center, the computers signed in for thirty-minute Web sessions. Their servers blocked porn sites, so it was never busy.

"Not likely," Thora said, with authority.

"It's pretty old stuff, mostly," Ally said.

"Still."

"Not all of it," Thora said. "That one girl was basically a few months ago. At the Super Bowl thing."

"But didn't she just say he tried?"

Russell stared darkly at his plate. "That's just as bad."

Ally and Thora glanced at each other but stayed silent.

G. PUT HIMSELF IN charge of the puppies, or maybe Robert did; at any rate, all of a sudden there was G., squatting by the box in the common area, spooning cottage cheese into a bowl. Up until then G. had only seemed to interact with Robert, but now people were reporting conversations, G. chatting away with whoever came by to look at the puppies.

It was the first time Thora had encountered him mostly alone: there was a man playing solitaire at one of the tables, Blue Planet silently on the TV, but other than G., the common room was empty. Thora dropped her shoulders, ran her tongue along her top teeth.

"Cute," Thora said, squatting to G.'s level. "Puppies."

"Their eyes still won't open for another week or so," G. said. He glanced up at her; Thora strained to detect some sinister ripple in his look, but it was too brief.

"Is it okay to hold one?" Thora said.

"Is it okay, Mama?" G. said, directing the question at the big dog panting away. Bizarre. Thora kept a mild smile on her face while G. scratched the dog's chin energetically. "Sure," G. said, still looking at the dog. "Just let her see that you have it. That you aren't taking it away from her."

Thora settled onto her knees, aware of how close she was to G. He had definitely lost weight, but his face was still recognizable: the soggy skin around his eyes, the coarse stubble, the thick ears. His hands were immaculate, he wore no wedding ring. His wife—a former manager in G.'s restaurant group—had, obviously, initiated divorce proceedings.

Thora reached into the box, going for the closest puppy. It was warm, mottled with brown, the size of a burrito. She held it with two hands, knowing G. was probably watching her.

"That's the fattest one," G. said. "Though they're all pretty healthy. No runts."

The puppy's heart was racing, its head rearing around. Thora tried to hold the puppy gently. "Wow," she said. "Imagine their tiny little hearts in there."

It was something Ally had said about the puppies; G. murmured thoughtfully in response.

When Thora introduced herself, she looked straight into his eyes, smiling. "I'm Thora."

"I'm G—" he said, not smiling back, though he didn't seem unfriendly. Thora told herself he was likely being careful. She glanced at the man playing solitaire to see if he was watching them. He wasn't. G. scooted the bowl of cottage cheese closer to the dog. The dog respond. Thora placed the puppy back with the others, its little claws skittering on the cardboard.

"Eat, Mama," G. said. The dog was lying there, panting.

"Is she okay?"

"Just tired." G. spooned a little cottage cheese out with his finger. The dog licked it, finally, and G. brightened. "There you go, Mama," he said, "easy."

Thora stayed kneeling like this was all very fascinating. And maybe there was a weird thrill in watching the puppies nurse, the pure creaturely fact of it.

"She's been hiding the puppies," he said. "Robert found one in the couch cushions yesterday."

Thora had heard this story already but acted like she hadn't.

"The couch cushions?"

"I guess its 'cause she's trying to protect them, you know? Good thing no one sat on the pup."

"Yeah." Thora stayed quiet for a little longer but he didn't speak again. She got up.

“Nice to meet you,” she said. She cocked her head slightly, her shoulders back, readying herself for his gaze.

“You too,” he said. He didn’t look up.

IT RAINED THE NEXT DAY, a rare steady rain. The air went a bit blue: Thora closed all the windows in their room. The staff was taking a few of the vans into town, for anyone who wanted to go to the mall.

“Wanna come with? We can see a movie?” Ally said. “Or maybe we can get my ears pierced?”

“Sorry,” Thora said. “I’m just gonna hang here.”

Ally seemed suddenly lonesome, girlish, her fingers grazing her earlobes. “We’re gonna go to the bakery. You want me to bring you back a cookie?”

“I’m good,” Thora said.

Thora wanted Ally to leave, but when she finally did, Thora felt guilty. Thora took an apple to their room, ate it all the way to its meager center, and spat the seeds on the floor.

Thora hadn’t seen G. leave with the others,

but he wasn't in the common room, either. There was a girl Thora knew from group, knitting on the couch. She nodded, Thora nodded back. The puppies were mostly asleep. So was the dog. Ally said the dog had been carrying the puppies around in her mouth, her jaw closed on their necks. Thora picked up one of the pups—it barely made a sound. A little chirp, like a bird.

Thora put the puppy in the front pocket of her sweatshirt. She kept both her hands in there, too, feeling its aliveness. She got wet from the rain, walking from the common room to the residences, her sweatshirt darkening. But she kept the pup dry. The halls were empty. She let the puppy go on Ally's bed. It was blind, squirming at nothing, against nothing. It couldn't go anywhere, could barely wriggle forward.

Thora petted the puppy with one finger. It was nice to be in here: the rain on the windows, the hallways quiet, and this animal, like a little soul that had wriggled loose from a body. If there were such things as souls, wouldn't they be blind mewling creatures about the size of a burrito?

She didn't know how much time passed. Maybe he knocked on the door, first, but Thora didn't hear. And there G. was, standing in the doorway, in his baseball hat, his polo shirt. His face was agitated. When he saw the puppy on the bed, his shoulders dropped.

"Fuck," G. said. "We were really worried."

Thora sat up, crossing her legs. He had sought her out.

"Yeah," she said, "sorry. I mean, the puppy's fine, though."

G. took off his cap to run his fingers through his shanky hair, flashes of bare scalp catching the light.

"They really shouldn't be away from their mother." His voice cracked. Was he about to cry? "She's freaking out."

"I thought it was okay. I didn't know," Thora said. "I'm sorry."

"Is she okay?"

Thora looked at the squirming animal.

"Did you think," Thora said, "I would hurt it?"

"It just shouldn't be on the bed like that, she might fall off."

Thora had arranged herself so, if he wanted,

G. could look at her body, consider it, but it was clear he wasn't even clocking Thora. She let the silence grow.

It took Thora a moment to register his expression: he wasn't interested in her. Was he disgusted with her? As if she was the bad one! Didn't he know that Thora knew every awful thing he had done? Every darkness that hid in his heart had been exposed.

He moved to pick up the puppy.

Thora held it to her chest.

"You're not supposed to be in the women's dorm," Thora said. Her voice was cold.

At the tone of her voice, G. stopped, suddenly, his hands flopping at his sides.

"I was just," G. said. "The girl told me you took the puppy and the dog was just, you know, really freaking."

"You should not fucking be in here."

AFTER ROBERT ARRIVED, furious to find G. in the women's dorm, G. had been classified as a more serious case and shuffled to an all-men's program in New Mexico. Thora recounted the story at dinner, Ally slowly chewing at her bottom lip.

"My heart was beating so hard. I was actually"—Thora lowered her voice—"terrified."

"Poor girl," Russell said. "You shouldn't have to deal with this."

"I mean," Ally said, "he's doing this stuff even here?"

"He shouldn't have come into your room."

"I honestly don't know," Thora said, "what he would have done if Robert hadn't shown up."

Russell massaged Thora's shoulder, Ally leaning against her. "We're just glad," Ally said, "that you're okay."

Their faces were concerned, their voices soothing, but, Thora noticed, their eyes were bright.

THAT SUMMER, THORA—returned to her home, returned to her life—finally read the book about the dollmaker in World War II: Ally had been right. It was a great book. Thora cried when the dollmaker's daughter found the carved birdhouse in the attic, proof that her Nazi lover remembered her after all. Thora read the last scene aloud to herself, the buzz of June beyond the windows of the house, the house where she lived with her husband, and there was something in the book that made being a different sort of person seem possible. It was a book about people, how people should help each other, and really, wasn't that what life was about? Weren't people basically good?

She resolved not to go on the chatroom.

She resolved to brush her teeth before James got home.

The feeling lasted for a little while. Then James was late for dinner, and there, in the dining room, the sky outside going dark, whatever she had felt earlier was already slipping away, already gone.

James was looking at her.

"What?" Thora said. "Did you say something?"

James shook his head, shrugged. He had a sty making its angry way to the surface, swelling his eyelid unpleasantly.

They watched the news in bed, James holding a warm tea bag to his eye. G. had declared bankruptcy. G. had avoided criminal charges but was due to appear in court for a scheduling conference for the first civil case the next week. There was footage of him, harried, exiting a car, a benzodiazepine smile on his face.

James put the tea bag on the nightstand. His eye looked just as red, only now the surrounding area was damp, too, the skin puckered by heat and moisture.

His hand crept toward his swollen eye, then paused in midair. She saw his desire to do something, to scratch his infected eye, then saw him understand that he should not, saw him remember that he had been told, expressly, not to touch his eye. And for James, that was enough—he did not do the thing he wanted to do, his hand dropping back to the blanket. Instead, James blinked hard, blinked deliberately. He smiled at her, a tear dripping from the eye he offered to her for inspection.

"Any better?"

ACKNOWLEDGMENTS

THANK YOU TO Bill Clegg and everyone at The Clegg Agency.

Many thanks to Kate Medina for wise guidance, and to Gina Centrello and the team at Random House. Thank you, also, to Poppy Hampson and Chatto and Windus.

I'm indebted to the editors of the publications where these stories first appeared: Lorin Stein and Emily Nemens at **The Paris Review,** Sigrid Rausing at **Granta,** and Willing Davidson at **The New Yorker.** Willing has been an especially generous editor and friend.

For early feedback on these stories, I'm grateful to Alexander Benaim, Hilary Cline, David Gilbert, John McElwee, Spike Jonze, and Ben Metcalf. Thank you to friends Lexi Freiman, Tom Schmidt, Sara Freeman, Alex Karpovsky, David Salle, Alex Schwartz, Ricky Saiz, Ben Sterling, and Emily Keegin.

I'm grateful to my family: Fred, Nancy, Ramsey, Hilary, Megan, Elsie, Mayme, and Henry.

ABOUT THE AUTHOR

EMMA CLINE is the author of **The Girls,** which was short-listed for the Center for Fiction's First Novel Prize and the John Leonard Award from the National Book Critics Circle. She received the Plimpton Prize from **The Paris Review** and was chosen as one of **Granta**'s Best Young American Novelists. She is from Northern California.